WIT OF THE STAIRCASE

BY ELIZABETH MAY

WIT OF THE STAIRCASE by Elizabeth May

A love that cannot be acknowledged...

Jonathan Redding is a British soldier in Austria, fighting Napoleon's forces when circumstances introduce him to the most attractive man he has ever seen. Having fled from his home when his lover betrayed him to his father, Jonathan knows that he cannot allow Major Ainsley to know how his feelings. He spends his life both trying to hide his love for his dearest friend while at the same time doing everything within his power to keep his friend by his side.

A friendship that cannot be denied.

Major Stewart Ainsley, Earl of Durnley, does not know why he helps out the young ensign who is thrust into his tent one evening, but he finds himself enamored with the unorthodox young man. Their friendship continues until he is forced to make a decision; does he choose to pursue a path of marriage and children, or does he spend the rest of his life with his best friend? And if he chooses his friend, is he willing to move their relationship beyond friendship?

For my mum

CHAPTER ONE

Jonathan Redding was fairly certain that his epitaph would read, "He is dead because of an idiot." Or at least that's what the truth would be. Whether or not anyone would still be alive to recount this day, he was uncertain, but what he did know was that Lord Stratham, also known as Captain Percy instead of Ensign Percy for no reason other than his accidental birth, was a complete and utter imbecile, and if Jonathan were to die today, he figured it to be Percy's fault.

Not, of course, that Percy wasn't following orders, so Jonathan had to spread the blame higher up as well. "He is dead because of several idiots," would therefore be more specific. "He is dead because of several aristocratic idiots," would be even still more accurate. The fact that Percy could not see that there was no way their little regiment was going to do anything in the face of the line of French cannons besides die, however, led Jonathan to placing the greatest portion of the blame on Percy. Percy on his very large, very stupid white horse, as if to call the greatest amount of attention to himself. He had his mount shipped from Britain, and a beauty he was, if not a little dense. Personally, Jonathan liked a little more spirit in his mounts, but he supposed a little stoicism on the battlefield was helpful. The cynical part of Jonathan's brain was fairly certain that the large white stallion was shipped over so Percy could somehow be immortalized in some artist's fantastical painting. "Look at how courageous I was!" he would say one day. "I led the charge that killed every single one of my men!"

Well, perhaps he would not brag about it. But as Percy kept trying to advance forward in the face of cannon and artillery fire, Jonathan knew that was exactly what would happen. As it was, Jonathan was very happy to stand behind this large rock and not call undue amount of attention to himself until one of the cannons got lucky and blew it and him to smithereens.

He figured it would be a quick death. Hopefully.

Jonathan wished he had a bird's eye view of the battle. He was fairly certain that if they could only double-back around, they could circumvent the row of cannons that were volleying round after round upon them. Not that he could get Percy to listen to him. Percy, the idiot, whose father sent him to war to "be a man." Well, if it worked, he was now a stupid man instead of a stupid boy. Percy, the captain who was granted his rank merely because his father was a Duke and could purchase his commission. Percy, the... oh, well, that was something. Percy was dead.

Jonathan watched Percy, a brilliant target for the French cannons and artillery alike, take several bullets to the chest before falling quite gracefully, his arms outstretched, backwards onto the ground. Before coming to Austria to fight the French (Jonathan still did not understand that part) and experiencing the horrors of war firsthand, Jonathan had often wondered if men died the way the paintings had suggested. For all of the death he had seen thus far, that was the first death he had seen accurately portrayed. He was certain Percy's father would immortalize his son in just that pose, Percy's brilliant horse standing stoically over his fallen rider. Probably too stupid to know he should run away, Jonathan thought.

"Oh, dear God! They've shot the Captain! What are we going to do?" a wide-eyed Ensign who was sharing his rock grabbed his arm, his eyes large. What was his name? Doogin, Dolittle, something like that. It didn't matter. In a few minutes they'd all be dead.

His epitaph would read, "He died without a leader." That was true on several levels.

"Redding! Redding! He's dead! What should we do?" Jonathan heard another Ensign yell.

Redding was a common enough name... they were probably yelling for someone else.

"Redding!" the Ensign literally fell on top of him as he darted around a rock and into him. "He's dead, Redding!"

Not someone else. "Yes, yes, I saw," Jonathan said, keeping his eyes forward. The line of cannons *did* stop just a few hundred yards to their left. If they could move their charge around, they may be able to flank the line.

"What are we going to do?" the Ensign yelled.

Jonathan sighed. It was bad enough they were all going to die, but at least the poor saps could keep their fear under control. At this point, however, if he didn't do something, his epitaph was going to read something like, "He died sitting around and waiting," or "Died while hiding behind a rock," and that would never do.

"You, Ensign!" he yelled to the young man, who came immediately to attention to the wonderment of Jonathan, as he was merely a Ensign as well. "And you! Do..." he mumbled the end of the last name. The young came to attention as well, despite his obvious green visage. Amazing what training will do, Jonathan thought. "We're going to flank the row of cannons. Do you see that rock over there?" Both Ensigns nodded. "Tell the rest of our men to start moving that way, and when I come up, run towards the cannons and attack as quickly as you can! Don't move too fast, until I give the signal, or you will warn them of our approach! Got it? Good, now go, and start telling the men to move!"

The Ensigns nodded and left Jonathan's rock, either to tell the rest of their regiment what they were doing, or deserting, or perhaps finding someone who should actually *be* in charge, and asking *him* what they should do. With the cannon fire, Jonathan wasn't sure how many men were left, either being dead and all, or having some brains and deserting after realizing that Percy was going to get them all killed. Jonathan gritted his teeth as a cannon blast took out some dirt very close to his rock. Now that he had made a decision, he really was not in the mood to die before leading the attack on the cannons.

His epitaph would read, "He died pretending to be an officer." Oh, well, there were worse things to be accused of. Seeing movement around him, he noted some of the men beginning to move to the left. Well, that was a good sign, he thought. If he was going to die, at least he could lead a charge- that was more than he ever really hoped for, anyway. Jonathan waited several minutes- well, at least it *seemed* like several minutes- it was difficult to tell as every cannon volley whistle potentially signaled his end. When he felt certain that the men had enough time to move to the designated area, he crept around from his beautiful, wonderfully safe rock, towards Percy's stupid white horse, who somehow was still standing among the carnage of men. He grabbed the hilt of Percy's sword, quickly unsheathing it from the scabbard that was tied to Percy's belt. "Sorry, old chap," he told Percy's dead body, "But I don't think you'll be needing this anymore." Percy's body did not argue. Turning his attention back to the battlefield, Jonathan made his way to the white beast, who did not shy away or make any other movement as he swiftly mounted (for which he was both grateful and disgusted at the lack of spirit in the animal). When

Jonathan yelled and kicked at the horse, however, he bounded forward, leaping over brush and bodies alike. They quickly approached the outcrop of rocks and Jonathan yelled to his men. Well, not *his* men. The men in his regiment. The men who were now looking at him as if he knew what he was doing, the poor saps.

"Ready?" he yelled, turning once to see the men and raise the sword in the air, then swiftly turned his mount towards the cannons, which were now facing away from them.

CHAPTER TWO

"He died of boredom," would be a mundane, albeit accurate epitaph. "He died of hunger and boredom," would be more appropriate, Jonathan considered, although he was not sure the army would acknowledge not feeding him. They could not really make his epitaph read, "He was a traitor," as his charge had been successful, by the by, although if he knew previously that leading a successful charge against a number of cannons and helping to secure the area would lead to his current predicament, he may have chosen to stay hidden behind his rock.

Jonathan sighed, knowing part of the reason he was standing at attention in the Major's tent (and had been, for the better part of two hours), was because of his lack of gratitude when the officers had come in to congratulate themselves on his charge. They hit each other on the back, and laughed and smoked, and, believing Jonathan to be wide-eyed and in wonderment of being in the same room of such important men, had invited him in as a quasi guest of honor, without the honor and without the courtesy one might grant a guest, such as offering him a glass of brandy that they were drinking, or a cigar that they were smoking. No, he was supposed to stand and pretend to be in awe of them for no reason other than he had stolen an idiot's stupid horse and ordered around some wet-behind-the-ears soldiers who had never seen combat before.

One of the men he believed he had offended the most, Jonathan thought, was a colonel who constantly blew smoke in his face and laughed heartily at his own jokes. "How do you see yourself in the army in a few years, Ensign?" the Colonel had asked, laughingly. "Do you see yourself as Captain one day?" He puffed up his chest and smiled largely at the rest of the officers, as if sharing a common joke. *As if to preen his feathers* thought Jonathan.

Captain only because he was not born with a noble birthright, and therefore could not rise up higher in the ranks, Jonathan thought darkly. "With all due respect, Colonel," Jonathan had said, "The battle plan as it was, I was fairly certain I was going to die today, so I haven't really thought much beyond that." The Colonel had guffawed at him, and the rest of the officers had joined in, although quickly after that comment, Jonathan had been escorted to his commanding Major's tent, complete with Major, and had been told to stand in the corner, but had not been given the at-ease command.

Major Stewart Ainley, Earl of Durnley and son of the Duke of Lennox sat at a desk in the middle of the tent, and merely went about his business as if Jonathan was not standing there; signing documents, reading documents, giving away documents to messengers, and receiving documents from other messengers. Jonathan had never thought of the amount of paperwork that might be involved in running a war. He spent some of his two hours determining how much paperwork he had himself created, and spent a short time thinking about other epitaphs. Certainly he could not have "He was a hero," placed on his own tombstone- people would think him very bigheaded for doing that. Perhaps it could just say "Died heroically," instead. That is, if he died out on the battlefield. As it was, Jonathan was fairly certain he was now going to die in this godawful tent. He again thought fondly of his rock.

But when he was not contemplating paperwork or epitaphs, Jonathan studied Major Ainsley. He had seen him in passing, of course, but had never been this close to him, he being an Ensign and all. Major Ainsley had dark hair, almost black, and dark eyes to match. His tanned face and square jaw were at odds with the more refined English features, but he moved with a grace that one might not expect of a man his size. Jonathan had never scoffed at his own height, at six feet, but he was certain that Major Ainsley would easily top him by an inch or two. He spoke in low, even tones, and used the same tone of respect to the lowliest Ensign who entered his tent to the highest officer (who happened to be the very annoyed Colonel who kept slanting glances in Jonathan's direction). Jonathan had to respect Ainsley- or should he refer to him as Lord Durnley? He could never remember. "Major," he was certain would be sufficient in this setting. And so, for the better part of two hours, he studied the major, and wondered if there would be any leftover stew when he would finally be dismissed.

"I must confess I am at odds with what to do with you," Jonathan heard Major Ainsley say in the low, soothing voice he had grown accustomed to over the past two hours.

You could feed me, Jonathan thought, his stomach beginning to pain him.

Jonathan heard the Major chuckle. "True enough," he said, "I forget sometimes to eat myself, but I should not assume others might feel the same."

Oh, dear Lord he had spoken out loud. Jonathan closed his eyes in embarrassment.

"Come, sit," he heard the Major say, and when he opened his eyes, he saw the Major sitting on the edge of his desk, motioning to one of the chairs in front of him. I suppose that equates to "at ease," Jonathan thought (at least, he hoped it was still a thought and his mouth wasn't randomly spewing forth what went on in his brain). He moved awkwardly to the chair, his legs not having moved for the better part of two hours, and he did little more than stumble before sitting as straight as he could.

And stared straight into the eyes of a Roman god. Or Greek god. Oh, who cared, this man was absolutely gorgeous. Jonathan took a quick breath, and trained his vision on a bit of the tent just slightly above Major Ainsley's head. It would not do for him to get hard now, not when he was blissfully sitting.

"He became aroused by a superior officer," would not be his choice of epitaph.

"... and how did you get Percy's horse? And why, pray tell, did you think you were qualified to lead an attack on the French army?"

Oh, bother, had the Major been speaking this entire time? He seemed to be ranting a bit, asking question after question, but not waiting for an answer. Jonathan took a deep breath and continued to stare at his spot inside the tent. He had years of such lectures from the vicar, so if the good Major thought to intimidate him by giving him a stern talking-to, he was sorely mistaken. Jonathan's back had seen the whip more than once as well, also courtesy of the dear vicar, so if the Major thought that would upset him, well, then on that account he was quite correct. Jonathan was never very stoic when it came to physical pain.

"Are you going to answer my question, Ensign?" Jonathan heard Major Ainsley bark.

Jonathan blinked. "Which one, sir?" he asked, staring at the Major's beautiful eyes. Oh, he probably should not think of them as beautiful. Captivating, maybe.

This time it was Major Ainsley's turn to blink. "Uh... why did you lead the charge instead of finding the next person in command?"

Jonathan felt a surge of anger rush through him, then tamped it back down just as quickly, to be replaced by a dull ache in his chest. *Thank you. Did no one in the goddamned army know how to say thank you? Thank you for taking out the French cannons, Ensign Redding. Thank you for saving an entire regiment of men, Ensign Redding. Thank you for not dying yourself and wasting the money we spent on your piss-poor training, Ensign Redding.* Well. Apparently "thank you" was not a word used in the army, just as it was not used by the vicar. So he would deal with this situation the same way he dealt with it back home, with passionate disinterest. Jonathan cocked his head and narrowed his eyes a bit. "Permission to speak freely, sir?"

Major Ainsley rolled his eyes and waved his hand in the air. "Please do," he said.

"With all due respect," Jonathan said, "Captain Percy was following orders. He was too stupid to realize that there was no way we were going to be able to take out the cannons with our small regiment, not to mention straight on. I noticed that the cannon line ended, and what our small group *could* do was circumvent the line, flanking them and rushing the line of cannons before the French had a chance to either retreat, regroup or move their cannons in our direction. When Percy fell, I could have stayed behind my very conveniently-placed rock, and waited for another captain or lieutenant or corporal or major... anyone, really, to lead an equally insane charge, or I could tell the men to flank the cannons. I decided to go with the latter. I told two of the Ensigns to tell the rest of the men to move in that direction, not mentioning to them that the orders were my idea, not Captain Percy's. When I saw the men in position, I got on Percy's stupid horse and rode as quickly as I could so we could keep the element of surprise. The attack was successful, and now here I am." Jonathan took a deep breath, his heart pounding not merely from his long-winded speech, but from the intensity of the gaze of the man in front of him. He was grateful he was not a spy or a double-agent, for he was certain he would confess everything to those deep, dark brown eyes. Passionate disinterest, indeed. He wondered what those eyes looked like in the throes of passion....

Oh, dear. That was not a safe train of thought, not at all. Jonathan trained his eyes towards his now-favorite spot in the tent and thought of the vicar. Ah, yes. That did the trick.

Major Ainsley stared at Jonathan a minute before pinching the bridge of his nose. "Ensign..."

"Redding," Jonathan provided, without looking at him. "Jonathan Redding."

"Ensign Redding, why did you think you were more qualified to change the battle plan than those superior to you?"

Jonathan's stomach rumbled, and he paused another moment before finally looking back towards Ainsley, answering, "That is an excellent question, Major. Perhaps we could discuss it over dinner?"

CHAPTER THREE

"He ate himself to death," would most likely be a poor epitaph, although Jonathan knew he did not have nearly enough brandy to inspire a headstone stating, "He drank himself to death." Besides, in his experience that usually took a much longer period of time than merely a dinner. Still, a fine dinner it was, especially if it were going to be his last meal. And the brandy was exceptional. It was a pity that Napoleon had a crazed notion of controlling all of Europe- it had become dashed difficult to find brandy in England anymore. Well, good brandy, in any case.

Jonathan swirled the golden liquid in his glass and stared over at Major Ainsley, who had eaten most of his meal in silence. Jonathan hadn't really cared- he had been too hungry to pay much attention to the chiseled feature of man sitting on the table across from him.

They were still in Ainsley's tent, although they were sitting at a small table, in two very comfortable leather chairs. His mind wandered to the thin bedrolls he and his fellow soldiers using on the cold, hard ground, and sighed. He should be thankful he was enjoying this fine dinner with his companion, not contemplating the injustices of the world.

"You are an interesting character, Ensign Redding. Tell me, however did you decide to become a soldier?"

Jonathan's heart gripped with terror for a moment as he remembered that horrible month, and he willed himself to breathe. He doesn't need to know the entire story, Jonathan reminded himself. "I had a falling out with my father," Jonathan started. Yes, that sounded good. *A falling out*. He had fallen, all right, although if his father were correct, his fall was from the grace of God, never to be regained. Jonathan took a large gulp of his brandy before continuing, "He was a vicar. *Is* a vicar, I should say. We... did not agree on many things. Things that were acceptable for some, were not acceptable for me. A vicar's son is somehow held to a higher account than the rest of the world, apparently."

Ainsley chuckled darkly and sipped his drink. "So is a duke's," he murmured.

Jonathan looked up and was met by Ainsley's chocolate eyes. They were assessing him, Jonathan knew. He drew a breath and broke away from the piercing gaze. "Yes, I can see that. Well, no, not really- I have no real experience with nobility. Our parish was small and our benefactor's estate was poorly run. But I *can* understand overbearing fathers.

"In any case, after my, er... *falling out*... I left home. I worked as a clerk to the vicar... my father, so my original intention was to see if any of my old professors needed a secretary or clerk. Unfortunately, the term had just ended, and when I arrived, the school had but a minimal staff. I was told to come back in a month." Jonathan paused. He had so believed that the school was his answer; his professors had always been quite congenial and he knew he would not be bored with so many intelligent individuals surrounding him.

"You've an education, then?"

Jonathan nodded. "Yes, I was a charity case," he said darkly. "I went to school during the day and clerked for the vicar at night. It was no Eton, mind you, but they learned us all right good," he said with sarcastic smile.

Stewart ignored Jonathan's intentionally poor grammar. "Where did you go then?" he finally asked.

Jonathan realized he had stopped talking, consumed with the memories of those first few weeks. It had taken all of his willpower not to succumb to melancholia, not to merely lay in bed and sleep, trying to forget the hateful things the vicar had said. In retrospect, he had twenty years of having hateful remarks slung at him, so he should not have been so sensitive to them that day.

"I took a mail coach to London to look for work. How hard could it be, really, I thought."

"I take it was more difficult than you anticipated."

"I had no letters of recommendation- I had spent the past five years of my life as a clerk for the vicar, and *he* certainly was not going to write me one. One of my professors might have, had the term been in session. But it was my timing, really, that was the issue."

"How so?"

"The Season had ended. Everyone had packed up and had left London, back to their country houses, or to Brighton or to Bath, or wherever it is that the rich go when they are bored with their balls or routs or gambling dens."

"I sense some hostility there," Ainsley gave a snort.

"Not specifically, no," Jonathan said, shaking his head slightly. "It's probably jealousy mixed in with a lack of knowledge of how your type live." He swallowed the last of the brandy and placed the glass gently on the table. He supposed it would be poor manners to ask for more; pity, that. He would like to drink himself to oblivion, at this moment more than anything. Just a few more glasses would affect his vision, and then he would not be able to see the handsome Major Ainsley, with his jacket slung over the back of the chair, his shirt sleeves rolled up exposing his thick arms covered with soft brown hair, his hair askew from ruffling his hands through it when reading certain missives.

"That is... a refreshing comment, I suppose."

Refreshing would be a cool swim in the pond near his house. He wondered if Major Ainsley swam. What he would look like with water running down his body as he walked naked out of the pond, towards him. Jonathan squirmed slightly in his seat.

Cold water. Think cold water.

"So what did you do when you came to London?"

Jonathan took a breath. "I spent the first week going to every employment agency I could, looking for work. But, like I said, everyone who might need someone of my services was gone. I had taken only enough money to live frugally for a short time, and when my funds ran low, I decided if I was going to die, anyway, it would be better to die serving England than in starving to death. And so, here I am." He waved his hands with a flourish. He did not, however, mention finally succumbing to the melancholia for weeks, lolling in bed, barely eating, until he had finally dragged himself outside and had coincidentally passed a group of men looking to enlist the destitute. At least Jonathan had an idea of what he was getting into; the poor buggers who had enlisted with him were taken in by the promise of free food and not freezing to death.

"How many battles have you been in so far, Ensign Redding?"

"Counting this one?"

"Yes."

Jonathan paused for a moment, as if to ponder the question. "One," he answered finally.

Major Ainsley narrowed his eyes. "One?"

"Yes."

"I don't believe you."

"All right," Jonathan shrugged and sat back in his chair. He really could go for another drink. It didn't have to be brandy. Whiskey would do. Or even wine.

"I have reports from the other men in your regiment who said you were calm and took directly to command."

Jonathan scoffed and rolled his eyes.

"You don't believe me?" Major Ainsley said, mimicking himself.

"No, well, yes, I believe you, it is just that I am surprised that you have taken reports from the other men already. I have never seen the army so efficient."

Ainsley smiled in spite of himself. "The army can efficient when we need it to be."

"Color me amazed, then," Jonathan retorted, the hint of a smile on his face.

"Ensign Redding..."

"Jonathan," Jonathan blurted out before he had thought. "Please, you know my life story. You may call me Ensign Redding outside of the tent, but I confess to hating not only being addressed by a designation, but also of being addressed by the vicar's name." Hm... that would be an issue on his tombstone. Perhaps he could merely have them put his first name above the epitaph, "Died without a second glass of brandy." No, that seemed petty.

"I suppose I can indulge you for the moment."

"I appreciate it, Major."

"Stewart," Major Ainsley said quickly.

"Pardon?"

"Stewart. As I am addressing you by your first name, you should use mine. God knows, few enough people do."

"Stewart," Jonathan said slowly, trying it out on his tongue. Stewart, Stewart, Stewart. Yes, he liked that very much.

"I think this conversation has gone beyond its original intention. To be honest, *Jonathan*, I have not had a conversation in the past six months that did not discuss troop movement, supply lines or death counts. I confess to being thoroughly being entertained by your forthright comments. I was not expecting to be so."

17

"I live to serve," Jonathan quipped.

"Do you, really?" Stewart said, his voice gravely. Oh, dear, Jonathan thought, he really did need that second drink.

"No, but you know what I would really live for?"

"I admit I have no idea."

"Another drink," Jonathan said, motioning to his now-empty glass. Stewart reached behind him automatically, as if he had dinner with lowly Ensigns all the time, and grabbed the glass container on the cabinet behind him. "All of the comforts of home," he said, pouring a liberal drink for himself and Jonathan. "Is that not wonderful?"

"Honestly? No," Jonathan answered as he moved the brandy around in the snifter.

"Really? You would rather be out sleeping on the ground with the regulars?" Stewart's eyebrows shot up in surprise.

"No, who would, really? But the truth is, this," he waved his hand around the tent, to the desk, carpet on the ground, and the small table where they were having their meal, "is humanizing war. Making it better. War should not be made better. We are killing and maiming each other. That is war. By allowing ourselves such small comforts, we make it more bearable, which in truth only prolongs the suffering."

"A philosopher, then? Or a proper vicar's son."

Jonathan shrugged and then shuddered at the thought of being compared to his father. "There is not much to do while sitting around, waiting to be blown up by a cannonball. One has only his own thoughts for company."

"You could talk to your fellow messmates," Stewart suggested.

"I have learned three things in the past few months," Jonathan said, "Number one, don't bother to learn anyone's name. There are too many men, all who look alike and dress alike, and they will probably be dead by the week's end, anyway. One's efforts to learn their name will be for naught."

"As Major, it is my duty to know the men who are in my command," Stewart reminded him.

Jonathan shrugged. "I am merely commenting on my experiences."

"True enough," Stewart said. "Pray, continue."

"Number two," Jonathan said, raising two fingers, "don't drink the water. More men die in war from disease than they do from being killed by Bony's artillery."

"And you know this, how?"

"Books," Jonathan said succinctly.

"Books?" Stewart grinned, raised one eyebrow and cocked his head to the side as of to challenge Jonathan's claim. Jonathan felt his heart jump at the sight. Dammit, he apparently needed more to drink- the brandy was making him want the man in front of him more, not less. It was getting more and more difficult to ignore him. Jonathan shifted in his chair again.

"Well?" Stewart prompted.

"Well, what?" Jonathan looked up and met Major- no, Stewart's eyes again. Oh, God in heaven he could get lost in those eyes. The candles in the tent were beginning to run low, and Stewart's face began to take on a dreamy glow. Jonathan wondered how it would feel to run his fingers through Maj- *Stewart's* thick hair, hearing his low moan as Jonathan slid his hands down to Stewart's neck and tilted his head up for a kiss....

"Books," Stewart repeated, drawing Jonathan out of his daydream.

"Oh, yes," Jonathan said, snapping out of his trance. "Books. Ah, er...." Oh, damn. What was he talking about? Stewart's hair? No. Books? What about books?

"You were talking about men dying of disease," Stewart prodded.

"What? Oh, yes," Jonathan scrambled to get back on his previous train of thought. "More specifically, published papers. The vicar was writing a series of papers on the subject, and how more men succumbed to disease in war than they did by being killed in battle."

"That seems rather... odd for a vicar," Stewart furrowed his brows and took another drink. Jonathan forced himself to look away from Stewart's wet lips. How he would like to nibble on those lips, to draw one into his mouth, and... Jonathan took a deep breath. This would never do. He had to get control over himself.

"Yes, well, his papers were discussing venereal disease," Jonathan said darkly. Ha! How ironic, considering his own perverse passions.

Stewart almost spit out the brandy he had been drinking. "I... um... I..." he stammered.

"Yes," Jonathan agreed, nodding. "I know."

Stewart barked a laugh. "How I wish I could have seen your research on that!"

"It was quite boring, really. Mostly numbers. But I'm good with numbers. And that, coincidentally, is how I happened upon number three."

"Number three? Oh, yes, three things you have learned," Stewart smiled. "And what, pray tell, is number three?"

"Number three," Jonathan took in a breath, "is that we are going to lose this war."

CHAPTER FOUR

"Killed for speaking the truth," Jonathan decided would be an unfortunate epitaph, but Stewart was looking at him with a combination of surprised horror and hatred that made Jonathan wonder if he was going to be thrown in the brig at any moment. He certainly would not be the first man in history to be condemned for doing as such.

"And what leads you to believe we are going to lose? Besides the fact that you are not out there, right now, leading insane charges on borrowed horses?"

Jonathan pushed down the smile that tried to overwhelm him. Stewart- he did enjoy knowing he could use his Christian name- was quite attractive when he was annoyed; his eyes sparked and his jaw twitched just slightly. Forcing himself to look away again- he was finding he had to do that more and more often as the evening wore on, as if he was being attracted to the man like a moth to a flame- he said, "You cannot win by playing chess with Napoleon."

"Chess with- who? What are you? Are you half-baked?"

"No, no, wait. Let me back up. I'll explain," Jonathan said quickly, holding up a hand. No mention of crazy... that was the first step, he knew.

"When I was a lad, the vicar and I would play chess. Every day, it seemed, and every day he would beat me. Soundly."

Stewart shook his head. "I still don't understand."

"Give me a minute," Jonathan retorted, a little too vehemently, he knew. He took a deep breath before he continued, "I so wanted to finally beat the vicar, to prove to him that I could. So I read the theories of the great masters, I practiced and practiced, and I challenged my friends and tutors and finally my professors to play me."

"And?"

"And I still lost. The man is like a damned chess-playing god," Jonathan growled, frowning at the memory.

"So then what?"

"So I had to come up with a way to beat him. I was obsessed with the idea. So, I finally did."

"You cheated," Stewart said evenly.

"Cheat in chess?" Jonathan remarked, surprised. "How would one cheat in chess?"

Stewart chuckled. "You have never cheated in chess?"

"That makes no sense. I don't even know where you would begin."

"The fact that you have never thought about it is so very refreshing," Stewart smiled, leaning back in his chair.

Jonathan frowned. "I honestly have no idea how one *could* cheat in chess. But in any case, no, that is not how I beat him."

"Then how?"

"I challenged him to a game of backgammon."

Stewart's laugh filled the tent and Jonathan had to grin in spite of himself. He felt his heart swell a bit.

Be careful of having your heart break. You know what will happen.

Yes, yes, Jonathan thought to himself. But he could enjoy this moment right now.

"That is... I daresay I would not have thought to do that," Stewart said, wiping tears of laughter from his eyes.

"Exactly," Jonathan said, moving his hand dramatically. Oh, dear. The room began to sway a bit, too. Perhaps he should stop drinking. Or not, who cared at this point? What was he doing, anyway? Oh, that's right- pontificating, as the vicar would say, "And that is what your dear generals keep doing wrong. You keep playing chess with Napoleon."

"And he's better at chess," Stewart filled in.

"Eggzactly," Jonathan slurred. Yes, he was definitely drunk now. Although his plan had worked- he could no longer really see Stewart across the table. Instead there was just a Stewart-shaped blur.

"So we should switch to backgammon," Stewart said slowly.

"You will not win using century-old battle plans, that is for certain," Jonathan said. "You need to change the game, or we are all going to lose."

Stewart did not comment, but sat, his blur unmoving, contemplating the small candle flame in front of him.

"And I really hate speaking French," Jonathan felt himself babbling. "My accent is awful. If Napoleon invades, everyone will laugh at me," Jonathan whined, putting his head back onto the chair. Oh, that wasn't terribly uncomfortable at all. In fact, he could probably just stay here for the next few hours. Or days.

Stewart sat across from Jonathan, staring at him as the young man began to snore lightly in the chair. He was an anomaly, that was for certain, but much of what he said made sense. Stewart knew that sometimes it took an outsider to see patterns that those involved in the actual fighting could not discern, and he had a feeling that Jonathan was that man. Wait, Ensign Redding. Well, *that* he could take care of right now. He pushed back his chair and swiftly got to his feet, holding onto the edge of the table as he swayed lightly to and fro before the room moved back into position. Damn, he should not have let Jonathan talk him into continuing to drink. How had he done that, anyway? Mentally reviewing the evening, Stewart could not pinpoint any one moment in which Jonathan had really tried to coerce him into anything, and yet Stewart found himself addressing an Ensign by his first name, dining with him, and then drinking to excess, all three things he never did. He briefly thought Jonathan could be trouble, but just as quickly put it out of his mind. The young angelic man who was sleeping in his favorite chair seemed to have no guile, no agenda whatsoever. He could not imagine Jonathan- no, Ensign Redding... ah, yes, that was what he was on his way to do. Stewart quickly moved to his desk, renewed with the knowledge of his plan, and quickly began to write, lest he forget about his brilliant plan in the morning, when he was not quite so drunk.

CHAPTER FIVE

"Death by hangover," was not nearly as original as, "Death by swollen tongue," or as accurate as "Died from puking his stomach completely out of his body." Jonathan groaned as he rolled over to empty his stomach once again. How there was anything left in his stomach, he had no idea, but the fact that the world was still spinning was certainly not helping. The events of last night swam around in his head, disjointed and without meaning. The only anchor to all of his memories was Major Ainsley, no, *Stewart*, the only clear figure in the muddle of his memories. He drew Stewart's dark face to his mind, holding onto the dirt underneath him for balance, lest he fall off the world entirely.

"Here you go, Ensign," Jonathan felt something hard and cool pushed under towards his face. Perhaps it was poison, to put him out of his misery.

"What is it?" he croaked.

"Water," Stewart said. "Don't worry, it's fresh. I know your issue with disease."

Jonathan sipped the water gingerly, then rolled to his back, throwing his hand over his face to block out the light. "Are we on a ship?"

"Are we- no, you're right outside of my tent, where you crawled about an hour ago to relieve your stomach."

"You're sure we're not on a ship?"

"Quite."

"Then why is everything moving?"

Stewart laughed. "That will pass. You don't drink much, do you?"

"I do, actually," Jonathan admitted. "The problem is, I just have no idea when to stop."

Stewart gave a low chuckle. "We will have to work on that, I suppose."

We? You mean I'm not being court marshaled?

"No, you're not being court marshaled."

Damn, he had to watch what came out of his mouth.

"So now what?"

"Now what? That is an excellent question, Ensign," Stewart said. "For now, you are coming back to the tent, for if I even thought of taking you to the infirmary, they would smell the brandy on your breath, and there would be too many questions I am afraid I just do not feel like answering. Does that make sense?"

Jonathan groaned to show he was listening.

"You will spend the day on my cot, making *as little noise as possible* until this evening, when I am hoping you will be recovered."

Jonathan murmured something against his arm that Stewart could not hear.

"What was that?" Stewart said loudly.

Jonathan visibly winced against the noise, curling into himself. After a moment he moved his hand slightly and whispered, "Why?"

"Why? Why what?"

"Why are you doing this?"

"Well, part of it's my fault for indulging you last night, and the other part, well... I don't know, to be honest. Let's just leave it at that."

Jonathan mumbled something else against his arm.

"No, I don't suppose my answer was very helpful. But we can discuss my lack of explanation later. For now, let's get you up before someone important comes along." With that, Stewart leaned down and gripped Jonathan's arm, quickly pulling him to his feet. Swaying lightly, Jonathan looked at him with saucer-like eyes. "Strong," he whispered.

"Yes, yes, that part comes in handy when being a soldier," Stewart said, and half-carried Jonathan into his tent, depositing him onto his narrow cot. Jonathan groaned again and rolled to his side, curling up again. "Hold on," Stewart said. "Let's get you out of your boots."

"Don't have to," Jonathan said.

"Believe me, I've spent enough time in your position to know that you will feel immensely better without footwear. Now roll over to your back. Good," he said when Jonathan complied. He spent a moment assessing the young soldier, who seemed older than his mere 20 years. If he had begun as a clerk for his father, that meant he had been working since 15, which was not terribly young, although Stewart was fairly certain he had still been instigating in boyhood pranks at that age. Hm. He should probably apologize to his mother. Shaking his head mentally, Stewart focused back onto the issue at hand. Besides working, Jonathan had also mentioned schooling, which boded well for his plan.

As he gripped Jonathan's boot, he noticed that they were not issued by the military- most likely in Jonathan's favor, knowing the poor workmanship of most of the footwear on his men. The boots were serviceable instead of stylish, but well made. Whoever his father was, Jonathan did not want for the basic necessities.

"All right," Stewart said as he pulled Jonathan's other boot off and left it on the floor by the bed, "Let's get that coat off." Jonathan groaned again, but Stewart merely picked him up by the lapels and pulled him into a sitting position. Jonathan moved his head slightly until he could focus on Stewart's kind face in front of him. "I still don't understand," he whispered, as Stewart helped pull his arms out of his jacket.

"What don't you understand?" Stewart asked, finally freeing the red jacket and gently settling Jonathan back down onto the cot as if he were infirmed.

"Why are you being nice to me?"

Stewart looked at Jonathan's large blue eyes, rimmed by bloodshot, so different from his own dark brown ones. They were staring at him, searching, Stewart knew, for an answer that he could not provide. Jonathan reached up one hand which Stewart instinctively took, squeezing it gently.

"I don't... know," Stewart replied hesitantly, and lightly placed Jonathan's arm back onto the cot. "I am going to be out for part of the morning, but I will be back to check on you if you need anything. Do you understand?" When Jonathan closed his eyes and nodded, Stewart continued. "There is water in this cup next to you, and a pitcher on the table. Drink as much of it as you can. Try not to make any noise. Understood?"

"Yes, yes. Understood," Jonathan croaked, waving his hand to shoo Stewart away.

Stewart smiled. "Sleep well, then, and make sure you're here when I return."

"I have nowhere else to go," Jonathan said simply, placing his waving arm back over his head. Stewart paused for a moment, not sure of how to respond, then turned to walk out of the tent, leaving Jonathan in peace.

CHAPTER SIX

"Died of embarrassment." Was that really possible?

Jonathan had slept through not only that entire day, but that night, and most of the following day as well. He figured that it was the fatigue of marching and eating poorly that had finally caught up with him. And drinking almost a full snifter of brandy didn't help, either.

Major Ainsley- Stewart- had been in and out of the tent over the past two days. Jonathan was not sure where Ainsley had slept, but he had not been asked to relinquish the cot last night, for which he had been utterly grateful. He would have been lying if he said he had enjoyed sleeping on the ground, in a tent or outside of one; there were insects and other animals on the ground with which he would rather not share his bed.

But now his hangover had passed, and Ainsley was nowhere in sight, and Jonathan did not know what to do. He had promised not to leave the tent, so he merely paced around it, finally stopping when he glanced over at the paltry selection of books Stewart had. He was not surprised to find one on military tactics, but he was surprised to find *Candide*, *Gulliver's Travels* and a few papers written by John Stuart Mill. It seemed more the library of an American than that of a staid British officer.

Picking up *Gulliver's Travels*, Jonathan sat down and began reading, skipping over what he considered to be the more boring parts, until Stewart finally walked in.

"Vertical again?" Stewart said, seeing Jonathan in the chair.

"Do you believe it better to be a Yahoo or a Houyhnhnm?" asked Jonathan, not looking up from the book.

"Whatever are you reading?" Stewart asked, surprised.

"Gulliver's Travels."

"Ah, yes the book with the little people. The Lilli-somethings."

"Lilliputians," answered Jonathan. "But that is just the first part of the book."

Stewart shrugged. "I confess I never got past that part."

"I did skip over some parts," admitted Jonathan. "Swift has a tendency to be a bit... wordy at times."

"So what was your question? About Yahoos?"

"Well, I believe what Swift is trying to do is to satirize those who believe in pure reason, by juxtaposing them against the Yahoos, who are the epitome of Hobbes' man in his natural state."

Stewart stared at Jonathan. "Do you want to play cards?" he blurted out.

"I don't know how," confessed Jonathan, setting the book aside.

"Don't know how? Why! That's just not right, man! We have to rectify that!" Stewart deftly picked up the book and set it back on his bookshelf, where it would hopefully remain forgotten for several years to come.

"If it's all the same to you," interrupted Jonathan, "could we play chess, or something else instead? I don't really care for the idea of cards."

"Don't care for the idea- whatever are you saying?"

"There is something more... honest about chess or backgammon. You have a strategy, as does your opponent, but you can see their moves. With cards, well, it is all quite... deceptive, is it not? I don't really care for deception." Oh, the irony in that statement.

Stewart shrugged. "I have a chess board," he said. "Although one day I must teach you whist."

Jonathan felt his insides warm with the thought of "one day." That meant the future, which meant he would see Stewart again. Unless they were all killed by someone else's idiot battle plan, that was. "Agreed," he said as Stewart brought out the chess board.

They were several moves into their game when Stewart stopped him. "Are you even looking at the board? You've lost your rook, your knight and I've just captured your queen."

"Yes, so it seems," mumbled Jonathan. He peered at the board for another minute before sliding his bishop over. "Checkmate," he said, and stood quickly, moving to the small table that housed the brandy.

Stewart, however, was staring at the board in confusion. "Well, so it is," he murmured. Glancing over at Jonathan, he said, "Pour one for me as well. And you only get one tonight."

Jonathan smiled and brought Stewart a drink. "Color me chastised," Jonathan said, handing him the glass before sitting down and circling the liquid in the glass. "Isn't it... wrong somehow to be drinking French brandy while we're currently trying to kill the French?"

Stewart chuckled. "That is contraband, my friend. Stolen directly from Napoleon's supply lines."

My friend? Be still his beating heart! "They supply their soldiers with brandy?"

Stewart shrugged. "Apparently so."

Jonathan frowned and stared at the glass again. "Perhaps I joined the wrong side," he said.

"But the British have much better uniforms."

"Oh, yes! Bright red! Bloody brilliant! Excellent if you wish to advertise yourself a target!" Jonathan quipped.

"They are supposed to strike fear in the hearts of our enemies," Stewart smiled.

"They strike fear in that the French are not sure if they have enough musket shot to kill us all."

Stewart laughed and slapped his knee. "Excellent point. Do you want to play again?"

"No."

"No? You don't think you can beat me again, or you don't think I'm a worthy opponent?"

"Neither," Jonathan said. "No, I believe you were merely lulled into a false sense of security when I sacrificed my rook, and when you saw my queen open to your attack you did not bother to consider what the ramifications might be- you merely saw the piece open and grabbed for it." Jonathan sat back and pursed his lips together. "No, no... I want to see your battle plans."

"My battle... may I remind you that you are an Ensign and I am a Major?"

"Oh, if I had any connections I could have bought a commission," Jonathan said, waving his hand. "Besides, you know that this is the very reason you've kept me in your tent for the past two days."

"Is that the reason?" Stewart raised his brows.

"Are you going to show them to me or not? While it is quite enjoyable sitting here, drinking your brandy and trouncing you at chess, I do not see what you get out of the arrangement," Jonathan forced himself to breathe through that sentence. He did not want to leave, to return to the barracks and suffer through the idiotic conversations of his messmates. He did not care about their current female conquests, women they had left back home, or what they would do after the war.

No, he wanted to sit here in this very comfortable tent with the most attractive man he had ever seen, and contemplate what color Stewart's eyes most closely matched. They were too dark to be called mahogany. He had originally thought them to be chocolate, but they were so richly brown he wasn't even sure if that was correct.

"Here." Jonathan was pulled from his thoughts and noticed Stewart standing before him, papers in his hand. "These are what you desired, yes?"

"I don't know," Jonathan admitted. "What are they?"

"They are our current troop movements, battle plans, and current locations of supply depots. Why I am showing you these I have no idea."

"True. I could be a spy," Jonathan acknowledged, looking through the papers.

"Then you are the worst spy ever," said Stewart. "Taking out your own cannons?"

"It could be a ruse," Jonathan said absentmindedly, reading a few lines before looking to the next paper. "I could have done that to ingratiate myself into your ranks."

"The French are most likely better at holding their brandy," Stewart smiled, sitting down.

"I do believe you have insulted British men everywhere," Jonathan murmured, "although I find I cannot argue with you." He paused before pulling a sheet of paper and handing it to Stewart. "Is this the most updated information you have?"

Stewart took the paper, reviewed it and handed it back. "Yes, we just received that yesterday."

"The information is more than two weeks old!"

Stewart sighed. "Welcome to the army," he said.

Jonathan frowned. "That is one of your problems right there."

Stewart merely shrugged.

"All right," said Jonathan. "Goodness. Our cavalry does quite poorly in larger battles, does it not?" he said, looking up at Stewart.

"They're fine for smaller battles, but seem to fail in larger assaults. They are quite useless."

"Poor saps," Jonathan said, looking down at the papers again. "I am afraid I am reminded of poor Percy."

Stewart snorted. "I agree with what you said. His horse *is* stupid."

31

Jonathan laughed. "I believe I was more upset over the fact that I was going to have to follow the idiot horse than I was in having to follow Percy."

"He was a dunderhead, you are right," Stewart sighed. "Still, even I am merely a lowly Major. Those plans come from much higher up."

"Was it short for Percival, do you know?" Jonathan grinned.

"No, just Percy," Stewart smiled.

"Still, poor sap," Jonathan shook his head, putting the papers back in order and handing them back to Jonathan. "So now is the part where you tell me why I am here."

Stewart's mouth quirked up at the edges. "You have no idea how the military works, do you?"

"It runs the same way things work in London. The aristocracy is in charge, making all of the important decisions, and the lowly peasants do most of the grunt work and dying for the cause. A few of those peasants crawl up through the ranks- or into business, as it were- and give off the impression that the inequity is not so overwhelming. As an Ensign, I am technically of the peasant class- I have no money, just as in the military I have all but no rank."

"But you have an education," Stewart pointed out.

"A fact the army did not actually find necessary," remarked Jonathan. "The recruiters were quite appalled to discover that I had never fired a gun."

Stewart's eyebrows raised up. "Never?"

"As a vicar's son, and then clerk, I spent most of my time in the rectory or in the church itself. For some unknown reason it is frowned upon to fire weapons in a house of God."

"Certainly you spent some time out of doors, however."

Jonathan did not want to think about the time he spent last summer, free from the vicar. "Yes, but regrettably it was weapon-free."

"You know how to ride a horse," Stewart remarked. It was more a statement than a question; Jonathan had ridden Percy's horse, after all.

"Of course. I believe that they take away your British citizenship if you do not."

"Probably where all of those pesky Americans came from."

Jonathan laughed. "Indeed," he finally said.

"Well," Stewart said, getting up quickly. "As entertaining as this is, I admit I do have an ulterior motive."

Jonathan swallowed. The past two days were the happiest he had been in over a year, his hangover notwithstanding, of course. He forced himself to breathe deeply... he may see Stewart again, one day. He would have to refer to him as Major Ainsley, and Stewart would look him in the eye, and then look away; pretending they had never spoken. Could one fall in love in a matter of two days? Could one fall in love if the other was not even aware that you loved him?

"Jonathan? Jonathan? I swear, have you been listening to anything I've said?" Stewart's eyes narrowed. "Did you have more than one drink?"

"What? No," Jonathan said, putting his empty glass down on the table in front of him, standing up. "I apologize, my mind must be elsewhere," Jonathan said. "I'll just be going, to... well, where ever I'm actually supposed to be. Not really sure where that is..." Jonathan mumbled. "I'll find it, though... eventually."

Stewart grabbed Jonathan's arm as Jonathan passed by. "You weren't listening," he frowned.

Jonathan found himself looking directly into Stewart's eyes, inches from Stewart's face. Listening? He could barely breathe.

Stewart let out an exasperated breath. "If you are going to serve as my secretary, you are going to have to start listening."

"What? You want me to be... you want me to act as your secretary? But... I'm just an Ensign."

"You honestly were not listening to anything I just said, were you? I said you were being promoted to corporal and you were going to act as my secretary for the time being."

"I don't... corporal? However did you make that happen?" Jonathan sat down heavily in the chair he had just vacated.

Stewart smiled slyly. "It was actually your impulsive cavalry charge. A journalist wrote it up in the paper, and the Colonel had to acknowledge your bravery. However, he was hesitant to give you all of the credit. Apparently he believes you to be insubordinate. Can you ever imagine where he got that idea?"

"Um... I *may* have mentioned that I was... unimpressed by his strategy."

Stewart shook his head. "Jonathan, Jonathan, Jonathan. That is not the way to move up in the army, you know."

"Oh, I don't know," Jonathan said, puffing out his chest in an impression of the colonel, "I don't think things turned out too poorly for me a'tall ."

"Yes, well," Stewart rolled his eyes. "In order to... keep you out of trouble...."

"Salvaging any more failed charges," Jonathan supplied.

"*Keep you out of trouble*," Stewart repeated, "I offered to keep track of you... as my secretary."

"I... see..." Jonathan said slowly. He sat back in the chair and crossed his ankle over his knee, drumming his fingers on his leg. "So... what would that... entail, exactly?"

"It is not a choice," Stewart informed him with steely eyes.

Jonathan shook his head. "Of course, of course," he smiled.

"You know, you're deuced lucky the journalist was here to recount the story."

"Yes, yes," Jonathan said. "Quite."

"If he had not been, I daresay you would be on the front lines right now, possibly right in front of a cannon. And the Colonel would be the one firing it."

"Is the journalist a friend of yours, or did he owe you a favor?"

Stewart threw his arms up. "How the dickens do you do that?"

Jonathan shrugged. "A gift. Perhaps I have Romany in my background. My non-aristocratic background, of course."

"Bah," Stewart said. "I didn't do it because I felt guilty."

"No? You made me stand in the corner for two hours," Jonathan reminded him.

"Maybe a little guilty," Stewart admitted. "To be honest, I felt some sort of... well, connection to you. As if I were supposed to take care of you or something."

"I'm sure you say that to all of your Ensigns," Jonathan joked.

"No, no," Stewart shook his head and began pacing about the small tent. "No, you don't understand. I should not think that. You were correct when you said that most of the men out there will die. I should not play favorites with one life over another. It's poor soldiering."

"The history books are filled with accounts of men saving one of their comrades in a battle," Jonathan countered. "They are recounted as heroes, even though technically they not only chose one man over another, but sometimes their insistency not to leave their fellow soldier to die put others at risk."

"Are you saying that to make me feel better? Because the paperwork is already done," Stewart said.

Jonathan laughed and slapped his knee. "Oh, this is going to be delightful! I never thought when I signed up for the military that I would have fun."

Stewart shook his head and sat back down. "You honestly have no idea how the military works."

"The rules are for those who follow them," replied Jonathan. "Now, if you would, set up the chessboard. I have a desire to beat you soundly again."

Stewart was not exactly sure why, but he did as he was told. Taking orders from an ensign- or even corporal? How the mighty had fallen.

CHAPTER SEVEN

"We think he died as all we found were little bits," was sadly a very fitting epitaph for most of the men involved in this particular battle.

After retreating- no, though Jonathan, correcting himself. After attacking, then retreating, then attacking, then retreating again, they had finally reached Corunna, only to be flanked by the French before they were able to escape to the British ships just off the coast. "To see freedom but not reach it," would also be factual. And sad.

He was tired of war. He was tired of Napoleon and his constant campaigns. He was mostly tired of being on the losing side of the majority of those campaigns, especially when it was obvious to him that those in charge were barely capable of piecing together an effective strategy. Let France have Spain, thought Jonathan, for all the good it would do them.

Jonathan, of course, was in the minority in that train of thought.

He was brought to the present as the man next to him fell back after being shot. Jonathan glanced over but did not bother to try to help- the poor boy had been shot straight through the head. Jonathan turned back and continued to provide cover fire from where Stewart had told him.

"If you see a blue uniform," Stewart said, "Go ahead and fire at it. Otherwise, try to keep them from advancing farther upon us."

Jonathan had stayed and followed orders, mainly because Stewart had been the one giving them. Still, he scanned the area where he thought Stewart had gone, looking to see how Stewart's advance on Stout's forces was doing.

Ah, there! Jonathan smiled. Stewart was leading a small group of soldiers to flank Stout. That was his Stewart.

His Stewart. Jonathan smiled. He could certainly die today, but all of the war and killing and watching men die over the past eight- no, nine years- was worth it to have known Stewart.

Even if Stewart had no idea Jonathan had feelings for him.

Jonathan reloaded his weapon and looked to see where he might best fire it when he saw Stewart surprised by a retreating French infantryman. They both shot, and both went down.

No, no, no, no, no.

Jonathan closed his eyes tightly and reopened them, hoping he would see something different.

His heart stopped beating when he saw that Stewart was on his knees, but still alive. Without a second thought, he jumped over the small incline and raced across the ravaged earth, skirting dead and dying bodies.

"Stewart!" he cried, pushing his way through a few men who had surrounded him. One of the men was wrapping a bandage around Stewart's leg, the thin material turning bright with blood. "Stewart!" he called again.

"Jonathan?" Stewart said, grimacing in pain. He glanced up with a dangerous look in his eye. "What the blazes are you doing out here? Did I or did I not give you a direct order?"

"It's your knee?" Jonathan asked.

"Yes," Stewart said. "Damn bloody frog got me."

"So now what?" Jonathan said.

"What do you mean, now what?" asked Stewart. "We continue the attack. Come on, men, help me up."

Jonathan pushed to the side. "What about me?" he asked.

"What do you mean? I-" he squeezed his eyes and clenched his jaw against the pain. "I told you to stay back, *Corporal Redding. Go back.*"

No. Hmm... maybe, that would not go over well. "Let me help you," Jonathan said instead, putting his shoulder up against Stewart's right side, draping his arm across his shoulder.

"Fine," bit out Stewart, turning back in the direction. "You! Burland!" he called to a muscular young man. "I want you to lead the men up. I'll be along directly."

Burland nodded and yelled to the men, who broke away from Stewart and Jonathan without looking back. War had that effect on men, Jonathan thought as he pulled Stewart's pistol out from under his coat with his right hand. Stewart glared at him out of the corner of his eye and gritted his teeth as he took another step forward. "What?" Jonathan said. "It's not like you're going to fire it with your left hand."

"What... the... hell... were... you... thinking..." said Stewart, forcing out each word as they half walked, half skipped across the battlefield. Jonathan did not answer, but thought back to the night which seemed to foretell their current situation.

"What the devil is Moore thinking?" asked Jonathan as he and Stewart sat in the small tent. He knew he was almost shouting. The campaign in Spain was nowhere near as comfortable as Austria, even if it was not as cold. "If he had any brains whatsoever he would just retreat back to Portugal and regroup."

"That's what we're doing," said Stewart.

"How is retreating the same as attacking Soult at Carrión? The last I checked, that's going the wrong direction," Jonathan said, beginning to pace back and forth in the tent.

"He thinks he can still join forces with Hope," explained Stewart.

Jonathan snorted. "He hopes? Excellent, he hopes for Hope. Meanwhile, Soult's forces are on our heels like sheepdogs and Napoleon is right behind him. And," Jonathan added forcefully, "it's raining."

Stewart watched Jonathan pace back and forth. He knew that there was wisdom in what Jonathan was saying, but after almost nine years, Jonathan still did not seem to grasp simple command structure.

Stewart sighed. "He is in charge of this campaign, Jonathan. I've told you, this is how the military works."

Jonathan turned around and threw down the orders. "And that is why we're going to lose. I tell you, if Moore continues to march towards Madrid without knowing whether or not Napoleon has already captured it, or if there are more forces than our admittedly awful intelligence is telling us, we will be in the middle of the country with retreat not even an option."

Stewart frowned. "Jonathan, I already stated as much to Moore and the other generals. I am outranked. There is nothing left for us to do."

"Damnation!" Jonathan yelled. "I don't mind dying, Stewart. You know that. I just don't want to die... stupidly."

Stewart smiled. "People die of stupid things all the time, Jonathan. Come, sit. Have a drink with me and we can discuss... less stupid ways to die."

Jonathan frowned but sat down obligingly. "I can't think of any," he finally said, kicking the table with his foot.

Jonathan was brought out of his thoughts by an advancing French soldier, who he shot automatically with Stewart's pistol before throwing it away. Helping Stewart was not a stupid way to die, thought Jonathan, even though his friend was weighing more and more heavily on his shoulder. I should have fallen in love with a shorter man, Jonathan philosophized. "Stewart, perhaps we should turn back, get your leg looked at."

"No," said Stewart, his sword clutched in his left hand. "I'm not leaving my men."

You'll leave them soon enough if you die of blood loss, thought Jonathan, looking grimly at Stewart's leg. "All right," Jonathan said. "Let me just see if this poor dead chap has a pistol we can... borrow." He stopped, gently easing Stewart's weight off of his shoulder, and turned the dead man over. To Jonathan's disappointment, all he had was a large bullet hole in him.

"Too bad," Jonathan muttered. "All right, then, Stewart, let's go then." He turned around, only to see Stewart unconscious on the ground.

"Damn it all. You see? This is what happens when you don't listen to me, you stupid..." Jonathan let his words trail off as he felt along Stewart's neck for a pulse. He felt his heart grip and forced himself to breathe as he pressed his fingers against Stewart's neck.

It was there, albeit weak.

"All right, then," Jonathan said. "Stewart, as your military strategist, I suggest we make a tactical retreat. Do you have any orders to the contrary?"

Stewart's ashen face did not reply.

"Excellent," Jonathan said, putting Stewart over one shoulder, grunting with the weight. "I knew you'd see it my way." With painful slowness, Jonathan limped back to where Stewart had told him to stay put.

CHAPTER EIGHT

"Insubordination" usually did not warrant death, but the major staring at Jonathan with rage in his bloodshot eyes looked ready to kill him.

He and Stewart were in Portugal, in a makeshift hospital in what Jonathan would consider a makeshift building. And apparently the military ranks were as important here as they were the battlefield, which meant that Jonathan as a corporal held the lowest rank of those facing him.

Jonathan *had* ranted and raved earlier that day, causing an outrageous ruckus. But how the devil was Stewart going to get well in such a hellhole? Unfortunately, the alcohol seemed to flow more steadily here than the battlefield, Jonathan noted, glancing about at the doctors, half of whom appeared to be drunk already at 10 in the morning. The drunkenness of the officers seemed to epitomize in the quite hung over major in front of him. It truly wasn't Jonathan's fault the major wanted to kill him, however; Jonathan figured the major had to take some of the blame himself. After all, it was because the major had been passed out drunk that he was in the battered state he was in now; Jonathan had roused the major to consciousness and then hit him in order to try to keep him awake. It was by pure coincidence that the General had come by randomly to inspect the hospital that morning.

Jonathan looked to the Major first, then to the General standing next to him, and finally to the small man in a cheap suit writing furiously. A journalist, Jonathan thought. That was unfortunate, indeed. Or not- perhaps the vicar could read about him being hung for assaulting a superior officer. It might brighten his day a little.

The General was a large man, about as tall as Stewart, but twice as wide. He had a full head of grey hair that was probably too afraid to fall out, and he looked like he would just as soon strangle his enemies to death with his enormous hands as he would shoot them. It was men like these, thought Jonathan, that inspired stories of Hercules and Goliath. Jonathan looked back to the Major, and realized that the disheveled man was more angry at Jonathan for exposing his drunkenness in front of the General than for hitting him. The General, Jonathan supposed, was more angry at Jonathan for exposing anything in front of the journalist. And the journalist was... well, he was still scribbling away.

"Major!" barked the General. "Outside, now. My carriage is waiting. You and I will be... having a discussion about your next assignment," he said. Jonathan was not afraid of much, but at that moment, he was terrified of the General, and oh, so thankful he was not on the receiving end of that discussion.

"Corporal!"

Jonathan jumped. *Bullocks.*

"Walk with me," the General ordered, and turned and walked out the door of the infirmary, leaving to Jonathan to trot quickly to catch up to him. He stole a quick glance at Stewart before exiting the room. The journalist was still scribbling furiously.

"You've left me in quite the pickle, yes, quite the pickle indeed," the General said as they strode down the hallway.

"I don't understand, sir. I don't see what I had to do with anything," Jonathan said innocently. It was the Major who had decided to crawl inside of the bottle and live there. Jonathan just liked to visit it nightly.

But the General did not seem to hear him. "This campaign of Moore's was a disaster! A disaster!" the General said, waving his arms. "And now... this... fiasco you've created.... Bah!" he yelled.

"I was just acting out of concern for my fr- my commanding officer," said Jonathan, catching himself. "I am personal secretary to Major Ainsley, and I am concerned about the sanitation here. I've read several papers on disease in hospitals killing soldiers. I tried to talk to the doctors, but they're mostly drunk. When I tried to find out who was in charge, I was led to the Major, who was, well... not awake."

The General snorted.

"I was just acting in the best interest of my commanding officer," Jonathan repeated. Oh, that would do nicely on a tombstone. A little wordy, however.

"What's your name again, Corporal?"

"Redding, sir."

"Redding, Redding. Yes, yes, I've heard about you. You, dragging that major two miles to safety. Newspapers have loved that. You're getting another commendation for bravery, did you hear?"

Jonathan had not. But, you remained in the military long enough, you either did something brave or you died. The odds really were in favor of either.

"I wouldn't take it personally, though," the General added.

Take it personally that the army actually recognize something he had done? He wouldn't dream of it.

But the General continued. "The army is doing whatever it can to throw a positive light on anything to detract people from Moore's stupidity." They reached a small sitting area and the General stopped walking, and took a breath. "So now, Corporal Redding, what the blazes am I to do with you?"

Jonathan wanted to laugh. Hadn't Stewart said the same thing when they first met? Although Jonathan did not find himself attracted to the General at all. Afraid of, yes. Attracted to, no.

"Put me in charge," blurted Jonathan. *What did he just say?*

"Put you in charge of what?" the General said, peering down at Jonathan, who wanted to do nothing more than crawl under a rock.

But he didn't. Stewart needed him.

"Put me in charge of the hospital," said Jonathan. "I can't do any worse than the Major you just poured into your carriage."

A muscle on the General's face twitched.

"Give me three months," said Jonathan quickly. "It would probably take you that long to find a suitable replacement and send him out here, anyway. You can tell the journalist that I helped you expose the Major, and that you were planning on having me take over the entire time. In the meantime, I can make sure the doctors are sober when operating... or... whatever it is that they do." Jonathan's voice got smaller at the end, but he prided himself on not looking away or shirking under the General's gaze.

"Why are you here, Corporal?" the General finally asked.

Jonathan swallowed. "I'm here to protect the interests of my commanding officer, Major Ainsley," he said. For what- the *third time?*

"Ainsley... Ainsley... damnation- he's the chap you pulled from the battlefield."

"Yes, General," Jonathan said. Perhaps the General's skull was not just thick physically, but proverbially as well.

"He's still alive, then?"

"Yes," said Jonathan. "They wanted to amputate his leg but I wouldn't let them."

"I see," said the General. He narrowed his eyes. "Am I correct in assuming that that was what started this blasted scene?"

Jonathan took a breath and forced himself not to retreat. "You are," he affirmed.

Then General pursed his lips and rubbed his face with his hand.

"And you want me to let you run this hospital?"

"Yes, sir," said Jonathan.

The General walked over to the window and braced both hands on it. "A year," he said after several minutes. Jonathan simply stared at him, not certain what the general was saying. "Ainsley will be well recovered by then," the General continued.

Jonathan narrowed his eyes. "Three months," he said. "That's all I should need to make this fiasco," he waved his arm in front of him, "running efficiently."

"Nine months," the General retorted. "And you resign your commission at the end of it."

Jonathan considered this for a moment. "Six months," he said, "and I resign my commission."

"Fine by me. I don't think the army can handle any more of the likes of you."

Jonathan took that as a compliment, even though he knew it was not intended as such.

"Six months," the General continued, "you are promoted to Lieutenant, and you retire at full pay."

Jonathan blinked. "I don't think you understand how bargaining is supposed to work," he said, confused.

The General laughed and slapped Jonathan hard across the back. Jonathan caught himself from falling forward, and grimaced only slightly. "I've decided I like you," he said.

Jonathan felt his lungs catch as he tried to draw a breath. Oh, good, he thought. Better than the alternative.

"Can't have anyone lower than Lieutenant running a hospital, now, can I?" he said. "Besides, I think you've done enough service to the crown without recognition. I like to reward my soldiers when I can."

"I... er... thank you, sir," Jonathan said.

"Yes, yes," said the General. "Well, I'm off. I have plans for Ol' Bony, and I mean to finally defeat the bastard. I'll look forward to seeing your resignation on my desk in six months... Lieutenant."

Jonathan stammered another thank you before the General walked out, and stood for several minutes in shock, reviewing the conversation. He had no idea how to run a hospital, much less make it more efficient, but if Stewart were to keep his leg and walk again, he would find a way. He took a deep breath and turned to the nearest nurse.

"You!" he said, "Nurse!"

"Yes, Corporal," the Nurse said politely. Jonathan had the good sense to feel guilty about yelling at her.

"I... uh... apparently I'm going to be running this... hospital," he said, "per the General's orders. Where might the office be of the poor chap who used to be in charge?"

"As you know," the nurse said with a hint of the smile on her face, "that *used* to be Major Boland. His office is... was... just down this way. Come along, I'll show you."

"Excellent, Nurse, thank you," Jonathan said, turning his charm on again.

"Of course, Corporal," she said.

"Er... it's Lieutenant, now, apparently," Jonathan said reticently.

"Lieutenant?" the nurse raised her eyebrows. "Well, you've done well for yourself. I should have taken a lesson from you, and started ranting and raving the minute I came in. Maybe I could have gotten more things accomplished that way, rather than just doing my job, day in and day out."

Jonathan smiled, not offended in the least. "Your candid remarks are what my friend would call a breath of fresh air," he said. "I do believe we'll rub along well together."

The nurse chuckled. "Here we are," she said, stopping at a plain room with little more than a desk, chair and filing cabinet. There was a small window that looked down across the grounds. "The Major didn't spend much time in here, so it's most likely out of sorts. But I'm sure you'll be able to whip it into service in no time at all."

It was Jonathan's turn to chuckle. "Thank you, Nurse," he said. "I do have one more thing to ask of you before you go. I'd like Major Ainsley moved to a private room at once."

The nurse smiled. "Of course you would. I don't know if we have one available, but if we do, I'll see to it personally."

"Excellent," Jonathan said, gingerly stepping over the threshold and into what would be his primary appointment for the next six months. Primary *after* he ensured Stewart's care, that is.

Chapter Nine

Jonathan was not sure if one could die by having one's limb ripped off, but if so, he believed his tombstone should read, "Lefty."

"Dear God, Stewart, if you squeeze my arm any tighter I shan't have any use of it at all. And I don't think I could convert to writing left-handed- I would end up with blots all over the paper."

"Sorry, I-" Stewart inadvertently squeezed Jonathan's arm tighter, and both grimaced in pain. "If you would just tell the man my knee no longer bends that way, I won't have to tear off your arm. Or, if it is all the same to you, you can switch sides of my chair, and I can work on the left side instead."

Jonathan frowned. "This is the newest technique, and I have it on good authority that if you continue these exercises- *Good Lord, Stewart*," he swore as Stewart's strong hand gripped his arm again. "As long as you continue these exercises you should be able to walk again."

"Does he have to come in everyday? I find myself- bloody hell!"

Jonathan closed his eyes as Stewart clutched his arm, panting slightly when he released it. He looked down to Hanan, the small Indian man who was lightly massaging Stewart's knee and rotating it, catching his eye. Hanan smiled and looked over at Stewart, rolling his eyes. Jonathan smirked, knowing that if Stewart realized the man was making fun of him, he would never agree to these exercises again. But he must walk, Jonathan had decided. He would make sure Stewart returned home as whole and hale as possible.

When the session finally ended, Jonathan wheeled a frowning and cranky Stewart out into the hall. "Where to, Stewart?" he asked. "Would you like to return to your room, or would you like to go outside for a stroll?"

"I want to go home," Stewart said sullenly.

"Back to your room it is," Jonathan said, turning right instead of left, into the private room he had converted for Stewart. It was bright and sunny, but also drew in a pleasant breeze, unlike his office. He dreaded having to go back into the cramped room today when it was so lovely outside, but he knew he must.

"No, I mean I want to go back to England," said Stewart crossly. "I'm tired of the continent, I'm tired of these treatments. I want to go home."

Those words were like knives, slicing directly into his heart. Jonathan felt the edges of the world collapse until there was nothing but his shattering heart left. Stewart would leave him and return to England. Of course he would. Stewart was an Earl- he would go to fancy balls and parties and get married and have children, whereas what would he do with the rest of life? His world, for the better part of ten years, had been Stewart. He was not certain what he would do. Perhaps the General would allow him to reenlist, and he could volunteer to go out on the front lines. He could tie himself to a cannonball.

"Jonathan? Jonathan?" Stewart repeated, turning in the chair. "Jonathan, why have we stopped? Did you forget something?"

"What?" Jonathan asked, Stewart's voice bringing him out of his stupor. "I apologize, Stewart. Um..." he looked around and spotted a nurse. "Here, Nurse!" he called, and she hurried over. He had not bothered to learn the nurses' names, either- they all dressed alike and had their hair all pushed up under their silly hats. There was no way he was going to be able to tell them apart, and they all responded to "Nurse," anyway. "Nurse, can you please take Major Ainsley back to his room? I find I... must be elsewhere right now." Without looking at Stewart, he turned on his heel and walked in the opposite direction.

Stewart, however, was still quite irate, and now annoyed that Jonathan had pawned him off onto a nurse. His knee was still throbbing from the treatment, and while Jonathan had promised him he would walk again, he believed it to be a fool's dream. He had not meant to lash out, but the thought of being stuck in this blasted chair for the rest of his natural life frustrated him.

"Th' Lieutenant's a good friend to you, eh?" the Nurse asked, pushing him towards his room.

"Yes," admitted Stewart, still trying to hold onto his anger.

"Ye should have seen 'im when ye first came in. Doctor, now 'e jus' wanted to amputate, but th' Lieutenant, well, 'e wouldn't let 'im near your leg, screamin' about who yer father was, an' causin' a t'rrible ruckus."

"Yes," Stewart grumbled, "I heard."

"An' when 'e brought in that foreigner- well, a few of th' nurses, they were ready to up and leave, ye know? But ah've seen more men walkin' now since 'e's been workin' on their legs than afore 'e came. An' things are so much cleaner now, e'en th' doctors are startin' to do more'n just amputate like they had."

"More men walking?" Stewart had not heard that.

"Oh yes!" the nurse said, wheeling him into his room and next to the bed. "Would ye' be needin' 'elp in gettin' inta bed?" she asked.

"No, I think I'll sit up a bit longer," Stewart said. "Perhaps by the window. Do you think you could bring something to prop my leg up on that over there?"

"'Course, Major," she said, moving a small table and pillow that was designed for that purpose. "'Ow's that?"

"Excellent, thank you," he said. "You may go," he added, staring out the window. He knew that Jonathan had prevented the doctor from cutting off his leg, but he hadn't really believed him when he had promised him the ability to walk again. He sighed deeply, and felt a bit of guilt creep up for having yelled at Jonathan, even when he had offered the use of his arm during the sessions. Jonathan had come up with the idea, saying that he had a much lower tolerance for pain than Stewart, and so would demand that they stop before the pain got too intense. Stewart was fairly certain, however, that he could literally rip off Jonathan's right arm before he would call out to stop the therapist.

But what if he could walk again? Have some semblance of normalcy back in his life again? He was not lying when he said he wanted to return to England- he was tired of the military, tired of the interminable war that never seemed to end. He sighed and stared out the window, his knee throbbing.

He was still sitting, staring out the window when a nurse came in a short time later with his dinner. "'Ere ye' go, Major," she said, setting the tray down. "Yer mail, and 'a've some tea for ye' as well."

Stewart looked up, surprised. "Where's Lieutenant Redding?"

"Well, 'e said 'e 'ad some business to see to," she said. "Do ye' want to eat in t' bed, or in yer chair?"

"What I want," growled Stewart, "is to see Lieutenant Redding. If you could fetch him for me?" He didn't add please.

The nurse looked at him in surprise. "As ye' wish," she said petulantly, and left. Stewart scowled. Jonathan was more sensitive than a hair trigger, and was still probably pouting about his outburst earlier today. It was more frustrating than living with a woman, not that he had experienced such comfort since being in this interminable hospital.

"You bellowed?" Jonathan's voice came from the doorway.

"Yes," Stewart said, "I need help into the bed."

Jonathan took a few moments to catch his breath before walking into the room. When the nurse had said Stewart had called for him, he had thought that there was something horribly wrong, and he had come running. Instead, he found a still-scowling Stewart sitting by the window. He wasn't sure if he was relieved or not.

Jonathan grabbed Stewart's chair and wheeled it by the bed, then helped Stewart into it, noticing that Stewart was less helpful than usual when being placed onto the mattress.

"Here is your tray," Jonathan said. "I made sure they did not give you any beets this time."

"Thank you," Stewart said, reviewing his meal.

"I'll be off, then," Jonathan said curtly, and made his way across the room, stopping briefly at the door.

"Do you want to play cards?" Stewart blurted out.

Jonathan shook his head. "You know I do not know how," he reminded him.

"You really should learn how to play, you know," Stewart admonished him. "It is all the thing in polite circles."

Jonathan snorted. "I am not likely going to be moving in those circles, as you are well aware."

"And why not? You're an officer now. Many hostesses love to invite officers to their parties. I believe they think that men look dashing in uniform."

You look dashing in your uniform. Jonathan shook his head physically to get rid of such thoughts. There was no use even in entertaining his fantasies, now.

"I feel I should apologize," Stewart said, breaking the silence that had fallen, "for my ill-tempered behavior this afternoon."

"You need not," said Jonathan stiffly. He wanted to go to Stewart, to tell him that he *would* walk again, that he just had to believe in himself as Jonathan did. But if he started on such a tangent, he was certain that Stewart would see through his façade, know why he was so interested in his well-being. Jonathan's heart fractured slightly at the thought of never seeing Stewart again, never touching him, never joking with him.

He knew that Stewart would never return his feelings; he never anticipated telling Stewart his feelings. Even when he had much too much to drink, he found the willpower to refrain from spouting his innermost thoughts and desires. It had been enough, he thought, to be around the man he loved; being loved back- either physically or emotionally- was unimportant as long as he could wake up every day and be with Stewart. Somehow the vicar's teachings had influenced Jonathan more than he knew, and in some twisted logic, on some days Jonathan found himself believing that his love for a man who would never know his feelings was merely penance for being born with such depraved feelings. On other days, Jonathan just found contentment while being in Stewart's company, and decided that that would have to be enough.

And now Stewart was leaving. Jonathan had not moved, but merely stood just inside of the door, part in Stewart's room, and part outside of it, a metaphor for their relationship. Who was he fooling, thinking he could spend the rest of his life tailing after Stewart? Certainly his friend would tire of him eventually, and eventually had finally come. "I am afraid it is I who must make my regrets," Jonathan said shakily, "I... I must review some hospital paperwork tonight and will not be able to join you for our usual evening discussion." Without waiting for a response from Stewart, he quickly exited the room, his boots carrying him farther and farther from Stewart; farther and farther away from the man he loved.

Yes, perhaps he *would* tie himself to a cannonball.

Stewart, however, just sighed and pushed his food to the side. Yes, dealing with Jonathan was definitely more frustrating than dealing with a woman.

CHAPTER TEN

"Died by overwhelming paperwork." Jonathan felt that he was slowly being killed day-by-day with the running of the hospital and its overwhelming needs. He needed a larger staff, but he found he would rather spend the little money allotted to the hospital on nurses, physicians and medical equipment than he would on a secretary and clerk. Jonathan sat back and put his forehead on the desk, banging it softly.

Yes, he had been acting immaturely last night. Stewart had every right to leave, to go back to England and continue his life. It was not as if he knew that he was ripping Jonathan's heart out, and it was not as if Jonathan could actually tell him as much. Jonathan had wrapped his head around the problem so many times he was fairly certain his brain was going to explode, but in each scenario he could only see one solution; Stewart going one way, and Jonathan going the other.

Perhaps he *would* just die under this mountain of paperwork.

"Lieutenant Redding?" a young nurse peeked her head into the doorway. "Are you feeling all right?"

Jonathan did not pick his head up from the desk. He was going to start banging at it again, soon. "Yes, quite," he said. "This is all the rage, you know."

"Really? How odd," said the nurse, and Jonathan pushed away the urge to bang his head right at that very moment.

"What do you want, Nurse?" Jonathan said, his voice edgy.

"Oh, dear. Well, I just wanted to let you know that Colonel Ainsley is asking for you again."

"Major Ainsley?"

"Er, no... Colonel. He told me he just got a letter."

Jonathan sighed and sat up. So Stewart was a Colonel now, was he? Well, just because he was a Colonel didn't mean that Jonathan needed to jump whenever he commanded. He should have the nurse tell Stewart he was not at his beck and call. That it was better that they stop being friends. That they not see each other ever again.

"Very well," he said. "Tell him I'll see him in his room shortly."

Sap.

Yes, he was a sap, but only for Stewart's dark eyes and quick smile.

"Oh, beggin' your pardon, but he's not in his room," said the nurse. "He's in the therapy room."

"Thank you, Nurse," said Jonathan. "Tell him I will be there momentarily."

Just because Stewart was in the therapy room did not mean he had to run to see him as he had yesterday. Jonathan forced himself to stand up slowly and close and lock his office door before heading down the hallway. He did not run. But as each step drew him closer to Stewart, he found himself walking more and more quickly.

Stewart was sitting in his chair, reading the paper, his bad leg propped up. Jonathan felt his heart squeeze at the sight of his friend, wondering what dark humors Stewart would have for him this morning.

"Ah, Jonathan!" Stewart said. "It says here that Stout is going to erect a memorial in Moore's honor."

Jonathan frowned, taken aback by Stewart's proclamation. "I don't even know how to respond to that. The French are... odd."

Stewart chuckled. "True enough. But here you are, then. I thought you had forgotten."

Jonathan knit his brows. "Forgotten what?"

"For my daily torture," said Stewart. "I believe I'm going to write a paper on how a good therapist is much more able to inflict pain than a French jailer."

"I thought you said you were done with the treatments and wanted to go back to England," Jonathan said with an exasperated sigh.

"Yes, I do want to go back home," admitted Stewart. "But I would rather return able to walk."

Jonathan frowned. "Yesterday you were all set to give up."

"Yes I was," Stewart agreed. "But today I want to walk."

"Does that have anything to do with being promoted to Colonel?"

Stewart laughed. "No, I received word of that yesterday."

Guilt washed over Jonathan. That was probably what Stewart wanted to talk about last night.

"But I must say, I am quite put out," Stewart said.

"*You're* put out?" Jonathan said quickly, his anger rising. Then, just as quickly, he tamped it down.

"I am," said Stewart, closing the paper and putting it aside. "For almost ten years, I have become accustomed to you being able to talk me into things for my own good. Last night you failed me."

"I failed you? You said you wanted to go back to England!"

"And so I do. And by my estimation, we will return on our feet, the two of us, together, in... two months and fourteen days."

"Two months... I don't understand."

Stewart sighed dramatically. "That would be exactly six months from when you accepted this post. Really, Jonathan."

Jonathan stared at Stewart, trying not to jump to conclusions. "You want to go back to England together."

"Hanan tells me I will need treatments for several months, even after I can walk," Stewart explained. "Who better to administer such torture than you?"

"I don't... I don't know what to say," Jonathan admitted.

"Am I incorrect that you don't want to return to England?"

"No," Jonathan said slowly.

"Then do you wish to return with me?" Stewart raised an eyebrow.

Yes! Yes! A thousand times, yes! Jonathan wanted to sing. And dance. Well, he didn't know how to dance. Just sing, then.

"I suppose," he said tentatively, trying to hide a smile. "But only if I am able to continue your torture... I mean, treatments."

Stewart smiled. "I wouldn't have it any other way. Now, call the therapist over, will you? I have an overwhelming desire to see how tightly I can grip your arm."

Jonathan knew he should not take that statement in the wrong way, but he felt giddy just hearing it. With a swimming head and a full heart, he turned to find Hanan.

CHAPTER ELEVEN

"Died of happiness" would most likely be too cheerful to put on a tombstone, but if Jonathan died today, he could definitely endorse such an epitaph.

It was more like seven months, not six, that Jonathan stayed as administrator of the hospital, finally threatening to walk out before the army sent him a replacement. He hoped that some of the protocols he started would remain in place, but he cared more for the thought of returning to England with Stewart than he did in whether the hospital ran effectively in his absence.

Now, Jonathan found himself lounging in Stewart's lavish townhome, rightfully his as the Earl of Durnley, complete with servants, and, now, a tea cart.

"Thank you, Mrs. Banks," Jonathan said, rising up to take the tea cart that the housekeeper Mrs. Banks had just wheeled in. He poured Stewart's tea before he placed two sugar cubes in his own, along with a hefty amount of cream.

"Here," he said, handing Stewart the fragile porcelain cup.

"Ah, afternoon tea," Stewart sighed, taking a sip. "Did Mrs. Banks bring in any cakes?"

"They're on the tray I just placed on the table in front of you."

Stewart took a few of the petite cakes, shoving one in his mouth before placing a few more on his plate. "I daresay I missed this," he said.

"We had tea every afternoon in the hospital!" Jonathan reminded him. "And on the ship over. And on the road back to London."

"Yes, but this is the first time in ten years that I've had tea *in my own library*," Stewart said, closing his eyes and breathing in the tea's gentle aroma, as if to savor the entire experience. Jonathan stared at the man in front of him who was holding a porcelain teacup with the same hand as he saw wield a sword and fire a musket. He never grew tired of watching Stewart, or of seeing him perform seemingly contradictory tasks with his beautiful hands.

The two sat in silence for some time, Jonathan nibbling on one of Mrs. Banks' cakes while Stewart shoved another three into his mouth.

"You're going to ruin your dinner," admonished Jonathan.

"Sho?" asked Stewart, his mouth full. "Ish my diher."

"Really? This is the great Earl of Durnley? Talking with his mouth full?" Jonathan rolled his eyes. "The aristocracy has definitely taken a hit. I believe you lords and ladies have a habit of marrying cousins a bit too often."

Stewart swallowed and grinned sheepishly. "I'm just happy, is all," he said. "I honestly did not know if this day would ever come."

"Having tea with your dearest friend? As I've said, we've done it many times before. Yesterday, for example. And the day before. The day before that. I believe- yes, I do believe the day prior to that...."

"Not in my library," Stewart reminded him. "The library I walked into."

Jonathan smiled then, as happy for his friend as he was for himself. Stewart still suffered a limp, but his knee was getting stronger and more agile every day.

"How does the knee feel?" Jonathan asked.

"It pains me a bit," Stewart replied, "especially in this awful English damp. But it's getting stronger. I don't think I'll be waltzing anytime soon, however."

"Or playing cricket."

"Fencing," Stewart admitted after a pause.

"Badminton," Jonathan returned quickly.

"Lawn tennis."

"Blast it, I'm out," Jonathan grumbled. "If it makes you feel any better, I've never done any of those."

"I find it odd that you received a formal education but never learned how to dance, fence or play lawn games," Stewart frowned.

"They did teach the students all of those," said Jonathan, getting up to stoke the fire. "One of the considerations my father put upon the professors when I was given a scholarship to the school was that I not to participate in such frivolity." He stuck the poker viciously into the fireplace, rolling the log to the side, before collecting his anger and sitting back down. "Riding?" he asked.

It took a moment for Stewart to understand that Jonathan was referring back to their previous tête-à-tête. "Ha!" Stewart said, spewing some cake from his mouth. "I believe I can still ride."

"Of course you can," said Jonathan in a conciliatory tone. "Perhaps next week we can go to Tattersall's and find you a nice, placid mare."

Stewart snorted. "We'll do no such thing. Unless she's for you."

"Perhaps I'll find myself a nice gelding, then, and you may borrow him."

Stewart rolled his eyes and made a face. "I'll see if I can raid the family stables, then. When the Duke died his will did not mention any of the livestock, and I know my brother does not need twelve carriage horses. I've been dreading going over there- I know my brother is going to ask me to help represent him in Parliament. It will be like the military all over again."

Jonathan leveled a look at Stewart. "What difficult shoes you must step into."

Stewart smiled slowly. "I'll see if he has a mare I can bring over for you."

Jonathan decided a change of subject was in order. "Very well, you distracted me, anyway, from what I was going to say before you shoved all of those cakes in your mouth," Jonathan said.

"They were good," Stewart smiled.

Damn, Stewart was beautiful when he smiled. The years did not detract from his looks, but merely added character, so he was more handsome now, Jonathan thought, than when he had first met him. He felt his heart beat an uneven pattern in his chest.

Jonathan looked at the clock on the mantle. How soon after tea was it acceptable to start drinking?

"So what is your idea?" Stewart said, bringing Jonathan back to the present.

"Ah," Jonathan said, glad to be distracted. "Well, as you know, I looked into your various incomes. They are... adequate, although I think with some finagling we can improve the return on your estate, especially if we diversify into both agricultural and animal markets. Specifically, sheep."

"Sheep?"

"Yes," Jonathan said. "Part of your estate rests on a very hilly area, which is virtually unused at the moment, as it is useless for farming. You could add a small herd of sheep with almost no downside. Or, conversely, you could try your hand in starting a vineyard, which is also ideal for such an area. The risks are greater, but so then are the rewards."

"I have visited that estate every year since I was a boy and never did either of those ideas come to mind."

Jonathan took that as a compliment. "The other idea is a little more far-fetched, but hear me out before you answer."

Stewart leaned back in his chair. "I would not dream of doing otherwise."

"Your investments are sound, although a bit conservative. I know the aristocracy is not supposed to do anything as gauche as run a business, but what if we create a front company, which I run, although you are the primary investor? With what I learned at the hospital, I was thinking of purchasing some companies which have been poorly managed, reworking their internal infrastructure, and then selling them at a profit. You, of course, would be a silent investor and would not have to be bothered by the day-to-day issues of the business. I would live here at first, of course, but as soon as you no longer need me to help you with your knee, I could rent a small office near the waterfront, one with apartments above it, living there." Jonathan drew a breath and waited, nervousness creeping through his body. Stewart just had to say yes- it would give him a reason to see Stewart on a daily basis even after his knee was healed.

"No," Stewart said with a frown.

"No?" repeated Jonathan dumbly.

"No," Stewart repeated.

Jonathan blinked. He had not been prepared for no. "Oh, well, then... I," he stammered.

"You make several good points, but I'm afraid I just don't think the arrangement will work as you've presented it."

"I see," Jonathan said, and stood suddenly. "I understand," he said as calmly as he could. No, he did *not* understand. His head was spinning, his heart was racing and he wanted to toss up his accounts.

"I did not protect you ten years ago, and put up with you all that time, for you to go live on the waterfront."

"Pardon?" Jonathan asked, not quite hearing Stewart.

"Jonathan, you look like a deer I've just sighted," Stewart said sadly. "What I'm trying to say is that I want you to live here, in this house. You are settled into the guest bedroom already. There is plenty of room- we can convert one of the spare bedrooms into an office or study for you; I prefer to do my work in the library. Work that will include whatever business you're working on, by the by. Last I checked, I am a retired Colonel in the British army; you should give me some credit. I may be an aristocrat but I *can* add and subtract figures. I'm not an idiot."

Jonathan felt the blood rush to his head. Live with Stewart in his townhome? See him every day? "You want me to continue to live here?" Jonathan felt shaky.

Stewart drew an exasperated breath. "Dear God, Jonathan, I don't know why you're constantly amazed that I would want to be around you. Am I the only one who has ever been kind to you?"

Jonathan thought for a moment. "Yes," he said, slowly sinking back down to the soft cushions.

"The more fools they," Stewart sighed. "Besides, I am getting the better end of the bargain. I get a therapist, valet, secretary and man-of-business wrapped into one neat package."

Jonathan felt his heart sing. "And I get to constantly harass you. So I suppose we're even."

"Do you think I should call you my majordomo?" Stewart asked, sniffing at the remnants of his cold tea. He grimaced and set it back down. He looked at the tray expectedly.

"You ate them all," Jonathan admonished. "But to answer your question, I'd rather not. I would think I were still in the military."

"But you would have gone up in rank. Major, instead of lieutenant."

"I never wanted to be promoted past corporal," Jonathan sighed.

"Well, what should I call you, then?"

"What you've called me since we first met," Jonathan said. "Your friend."

Stewart smiled and reached over to take the cake that Jonathan had left on his plate. "I can do that," he said, munching happily on the cake.

CHAPTER TWELVE

"He died confused," would be an apt epitaph, but it would most likely confuse anyone else who read the tombstone as well.

Jonathan was sitting in Stewart's library, ensconced in what was now considered to be *his* chair by the fire, reading. He had his usual late afternoon/early evening brandy in one hand, his book in the other. More specifically, he had the dictionary open, and had been looking up "love," somehow hoping to help solve the dilemma of his aching heart. Five years had passed since he and Stewart had returned to England, and Jonathan was as overwhelmed by his feelings as ever. He would say that he loved Stewart with the same passion as he had when they first met, but that was not true; instead, his love had spread, blossoming into something deeper than friendship. Still, there was no physical love; Jonathan had to fall back upon his daydreams for such visions. How his heart could be so taken with Stewart with no physical manifestation of his desire, he had no idea, and the thought of going elsewhere to satisfy his lust was unappealing. To compound the issue, he had no one he could talk to regarding the situation; friends of Stewart's would find him repulsive and while there were always whispers of some debauched men engaging in such acts, the majority of the stories were graphic and vile, not what Jonathan would consider love. They were not anything like the experience he had had when he was young, and not anything that he had *thought* he and his young lover had shared. Most of the books he had procured on the subject of men loving were merely instructional or visual in nature, and had no real reference to anything beyond the physical. He had turned to Stewart's library in frustration, but it was filled mostly with historical or scientific texts. The dictionary, blast it, was no help to him at all.

"Would you rather be loved or cherished?" Jonathan called out from behind his chair.

Stewart sat behind his desk in his study, reviewing the last bit of legislation for Parliament. He was overwhelmed with happiness that his brother was finally going to be taking over the position; he would rather face down an entire French artillery force than have to deal with bickering English lords one more time.

"Would I rather be... what?" Stewart replied, distracted. He looked up, but Jonathan was hidden behind the large chair.

"Loved or cherished," Jonathan's disembodied voice called back, "Which one?"

"I don't... aren't they the same thing?"

"That's what this says," Jonathan said, standing up and walking over to the desk, "but I beg to differ. I believe one can be loved without being cherished, but to be cherished one has to be loved. So it would be better to be cherished, don't you think?" He sat down against the edge of the desk and stared at Stewart.

Stewart blinked. "What are you reading?" he asked.

"The dictionary, of course."

"Of... the dictionary. You're reading the dictionary."

"As you see," Jonathan said, raising the book in his hand. "So, do you agree?"

"Yes, I picked that book up last week," Stewart shook his head. "The plot line was a bit thin."

"I looked up love," Jonathan said, ignoring Stewart, "and as a synonym it had 'cherished.' But as I've said, I don't really think they're equal."

"Character development was awful. And it moved deucedly slow."

"So you agree, then?" Jonathan said, closing the book with one hand and staring at Stewart over the desk.

"It was better than that Radcliff novel you purchased the other week, however, I admit."

"That was Mrs. Banks' and you well know it," Jonathan retorted. "But back to my issue."

Stewart shrugged. "I think it would be better to be both, I suppose."

"Agreed," said Jonathan, "Although I still say that one has to be loved to be cherished. But in any case you acknowledge they're not the same."

"No."

"You don't agree?"

"No, I... I agree with you that they're not the same." Corn laws were easier to navigate than Jonathan's train of thought.

"Nor do I," Jonathan said, pushing himself back to his feet. "And I am going to write the editors of the dictionary now and let them know."

"Of course you are," Stewart said, but smiled in spite of himself.

"You don't think I should?" Jonathan asked, looking back at Stewart.

Stewart mentally sighed. He knew that for all of his pomp, Jonathan could be overly sensitive, especially when Stewart's opinion was involved. "Do you believe it to be an important error?" he asked patiently.

"Of course. Who knows how many people will be using this dictionary, and confusing the two words."

"Then you should."

"All right then, I will."

"And, Jonathan?" Stewart said as Jonathan walked back across to his chair?

"Hmm?"

"Do you think we could read something besides the dictionary tonight?"

Jonathan's mouth twitched up at the side. "The plotline *is* rather thin."

Stewart chuckled and went back to reviewing corn laws.

CHAPTER THIRTEEN

"Died from oversleeping." Jonathan smiled at his own humor.

He had definitely overslept, however, and felt like the dead. His limbs were heavy and his head was fuzzy. He hadn't had that much to drink last night, so he was not sure what his problem was. Still, it was an effort to get himself up and out of bed.

When he finally dressed and walked downstairs, he found Stewart already gone to his club. Jonathan had gone as a guest there several times, but as he did not gamble, play cards, or discuss his latest mistress, he often found himself bored, to the point that Stewart visited it almost exclusively alone. This morning Jonathan was thankful for the peace, as his head was pounding, and his stomach was unsettled.

Roberts met him at the sun room, where Jonathan usually took the paper and had breakfast. "The usual, today, Lieutenant?" he asked.

"No," Jonathan said, turning a bit green at the thought of greasy sausage and eggs. "Perhaps just some toast today. I'm not quite feeling the thing."

Roberts nodded and returned with Jonathan's breakfast, leaving him alone, as Jonathan preferred. Although Stewart was an Earl, Jonathan did not understand the need for individuals to huddle over him, or to stand at attention in the corner, anticipating his every need. He had enough of standing at attention in the military- the thought of making another do such a thing bothered his heart.

Speaking of heart... Jonathan rubbed his chest absentmindedly. There had been a dull ache that he could only assume was from indulging in too many rich foods, which would also explain his lack of appetite today. He and Stewart had been out almost every night that week, and Jonathan was just not used to dining out so often. Perhaps he would beg off from a few of the engagements until he felt more like himself.

Jonathan choked down his toast and read the paper- at least, the articles he could get through. Were all reporters required to be such idiots? Some were definitely interested in reporting more of the facts, highlighting injustices and calling to attention issues otherwise neglected. Most of the reporters, however, seemed to make up their facts, ignore injustices and call to attention gossip and innuendo. Jonathan damned them all silently to hell, conveniently forgetting the journalists who had helped his military career. Folding the paper next to his empty plate, Jonathan stood up in a huff, deciding to spend the afternoon in his study, doing something useful.

Stewart found him there a few hours later, sitting back in his chair, staring out the window. "Working hard?" he joked, walking in and standing next to the large window. Jonathan had chosen this room for his study because of these windows, and Stewart always found himself jealous of the idea.

"No," Jonathan said absentmindedly.

"No? That's not like you," said Stewart, looking concerned. "Are you ill?"

"I don't feel ill," said Jonathan slowly. "I just feel... odd."

"Odd?"

"Yes, odd." He paused, then said, "We have a ball tonight, yes?"

"Yes," said Stewart. "My brother will be there, and I have been asked to attend. And you must come with me, otherwise I will be flanked on all sides with debutants." He smiled, but Jonathan did not meet his gaze.

"Of course," he said, still staring out the window. "I think... I think I will just go lie down until it is time to get ready," he told Stewart, but did not move from his chair.

"Jonathan?"

"Yes?"

"You are coming tonight, yes?"

"If you wish."

"I do," Stewart said. "Come, a nap is probably just what you need." He held out a hand and Jonathan took it automatically, pulling himself up out of the chair. "Honestly," Jonathan said, "I do just feel... odd."

"You're not getting out of going tonight that easily. You're probably just tired. If we were doing things full-swing, we would be going to four or five balls a night."

"Four or five? Dear God, I can barely get through one," Jonathan said.

"Which is why we only go to one," Stewart laughed. "That, and it pains me to stand for more than a few hours at a time."

"I thank heaven for your bad knee every day," Jonathan smiled.

"I'm sure you do. Which reminds me, I believe we can skip the massage this evening, and let you sleep a bit longer."

"If you insist," Jonathan said, stopping at the door to his room. "Thank you, Stewart. Can you have Roberts send a footman when it's time to get ready?"

Stewart sketched a short bow. "Of course, sir," he smiled.

Jonathan rolled his eyes, but quickly toed off his shoes and pulled off his coat, throwing it haphazardly onto the chair. He fell into bed and was asleep almost instantly.

When Jonathan was roused later that afternoon by a footman, however, he felt immensely better. He shaved and dressed in his uniform, then wandered over to Stewart's room to do the same for him.

"I must commend you on your ability to play both secretary and valet," said Stewart as Jonathan helped him pull on his coat of blue superfine. Jonathan felt a twinge in his left arm as he pulled on Stewart's sleeve- he was certain his tailor had made his coat a little too tight.

"I have been meaning to talk to you about that," said Jonathan, sitting down on a small settee next to the window, drinking a brandy he had brought up from below. "I think you should pay me for both jobs."

Stewart looked over to Jonathan to see if he was in earnest. Jonathan was staring out the window, his eyes glassy and distant. "I believe you cost me a valet's salary in brandy," he said, adjusting the cravat Jonathan had tied.

Jonathan studied his glass. "Perhaps so," he nodded. "Very well, then instead of money, I demand greater respect."

Stewart laughed. "As soon as you learn your place," he retorted.

"Damn," said Jonathan and sighed audibly. "I suppose we will just have to keep things as they are then." In all things, Jonathan said silently to himself.

"I suppose we will," Stewart agreed. "Come, I only want to be late enough so we don't have to go through the blasted receiving line, not late enough to draw notice."

CHAPTER FOURTEEN

"Died of suffocation" would not be an epitaph that would necessarily call to mind ballrooms, but Jonathan was fairly certain he was going to die from being pressed on all sides by masses of overly dressed snobs.

"Dear God!" he exclaimed as they finally forced their way into the ballroom. "Now I understand why they call it a crush!"

"Or a squeeze," said Stewart.

"Yes," said Jonathan absently. "So, now we are here. Do you want to stay and watch the dancing, or did you want to retire to the card room?"

"In a rush to get through the evening?" he asked.

"No," said Jonathan. *Yes.* He grabbed two glasses of champagne from a passing waiter. "Here," he said, handing one to Stewart, who took it without remark.

"Ah, there is the Earl and his lapdog," a voice said from behind them.

Stewart rolled his eyes. "Ah, Northumberland," he said, but did not extend the greeting.

The Duke of Northumberland, Stewart had reminded Jonathan when they arrived back in London, was Percy's father. For some reason he blamed either Stewart or Jonathan for Percy's dramatic death, although both were fairly certain it was the fact that Jonathan had led the charge on Percy's stupid horse that upset him the most. He was an older version of Percy- short, bald and quite stupid.

Jonathan, however, was not so polite. "A lapdog, am I? Perhaps I should lift my leg and pee on you, then."

"Still not married, Lord Durnley?" Northumberland said, turning to Stewart. "Perhaps no ladies want to be close with the smell of your company."

"I don't believe my marriage plans are in any way your business," said Stewart, turning away from Northumberland to watch the dancers.

Jonathan took the hint and scanned the crowd as well. "Good evening, Northumberland," he said over his shoulder, breathing easily only when the man stormed off.

"Why does he persist?" asked Jonathan. "Percy died 15 years ago-
he has grandchildren almost that age now."

Stewart shrugged. "Percy was his youngest. I'm sure he didn't send
him away thinking he would never see him again.

"Does he not understand the meaning of war?"

"He's a fat, bald, stupid man with a grudge, Jonathan. That's all."

"Doesn't give him the right to continue to harass us."

"He's a duke," said Stewart. "That gives him the right."

Jonathan muttered something under his breath that Stewart was
certain should not be said in polite company. "He married his cousin,
which is probably why his sons are so stupid. I should have told him
his family tree was a shrub," Stewart said.

"Or a stick," Jonathan muttered.

Stewart laughed. "Perhaps a caper. Thick and dense."

"Ah," Jonathan laughed, "such is the wit of the staircase."

"Wit of the what?" Stewart questioned.

"Wit of the staircase," Jonathan repeated, keeping his gaze on the
dancers in front of them.

Stewart leveled a look at him. "What?" Jonathan said innocently,
glancing at Stewart momentarily before flitting his gaze back onto the
ballroom.

"I have no idea what you just said," Stewart told him, then
narrowed his eyes. "Have you been reading the dictionary again?"

"Still," Jonathan answered, taking a sip of champagne.

"Still. So if you're at 'w' then I assume you're almost done?"

"I started in the middle, if you must know, and then became bored,
so I started to skip around."

Stewart rolled his eyes. "And you just happened to read 'w' before
we came here."

"As a matter of fact, yes," Jonathan nodded.

Stewart waited a moment, then two, looking around at the various
men and women in their evening dress, until he finally said loudly,
"What is wit of the staircase?"

A few people surrounding them turned and looked at them strangely
before turning back to their own conversations. Jonathan smiled and
sipped his champagne again. "Really, Stewart, you're making a scene,"
he chastised.

"You know what? Fine. I don't care," Stewart said darkly. "If I did care, I could look it up myself when we get home." Provided he knew where to find the dictionary. In the library, he assumed.

"Wit of the staircase," Jonathan said patiently, "is when you think of something witty to say only after you have ended the conversation. That you have thought of something as you're walking away, or more specifically, in this case, up the staircase."

"So it's something you didn't think of until later."

"Yes, I suppose. Something that you should have said but you didn't voice until it was too late to do so."

Stewart looked over at Jonathan, who now had a pained look on his face. "Are you still feeling poorly?" he asked. "Don't tell me you ate any of the crab cakes here- they did not look fresh at all."

"No, no, of course not." Jonathan laughed, tugging at his cravat. "Is it warm in here?"

Stewart shrugged. "No warmer than any other crush," he posited.

"Unhelpful," Jonathan told him. "It does feel quite warm. I think I'll take a stroll outside."

"Stay away from matchmaking mamas," Stewart warned.

"Matchmaking ma... really, Stewart, and you say I talk nonsense."

"You know I do not joke about that."

"Fine, fine," Jonathan said, pulling again at his cravat. "I'll be careful." As if he should ever be caught in a delicate situation. Ha!

Jonathan turned and walked through the double doors to the patio, which offered cool, crisp air that was in direct contrast to the dense, warm air of the ballroom. It was a brisk spring evening, and none of the couples had apparently wanted to brave the chill, so he had the entire patio to himself. Jonathan took a deep breath, his heart racing madly in his chest, and leaned back against the cool brick wall. What the hell was wrong with him? One minute, he was talking with Stewart, the next his heart was pounding madly in his chest. He took another deep breath, then another, and began to feel better. In fact, he was beginning to feel a bit chilled, but he did not move to return to the crowded ballroom quite yet.

Through the glass door, he could see Stewart talking to his brother, the current Duke of Lennox, and he breathed a sigh of relief that he was outside. Lennox did not seem to forgive Stewart for engaging in a friendship with anyone who was not titled, and Jonathan found himself pretending deafness to his putdowns in order not to embarrass Stewart.

They were surrounded by some of Stewart's friends from the club, and a few ladies Jonathan had been introduced to before. One was in a simple light pink gown and the other was in a more elaborate, but still pale, blue dress. Necklines were low in regard to the style, but nothing that would be deemed scandalous. They looked like children.

Debutants, thought Jonathan. He racked his brain, but could not come up with either girl's name. Not that he could probably name even a tenth of the people Stewart had introduced him to; it seemed his tact to forget everyone's name while in the army had continued into his private life. Jonathan mentally shrugged; if he never saw any of these people again, his life would not change one bit.

He watched as one of the gits took the hand of the girl in blue and lead her to the dance floor. One of the men next to Stewart said something to him, and he smiled and shook his head apologetically and motioned to his leg. *Probably encouraged him to take her out to dance.* Another git instead bowed to the girl and led her out to the dance floor as well.

Jonathan shivered again and decided he would have to brave the ballroom again; if he was already feeling a bit ill, he did not want to add a chill as well. Moving to the French doors, he made his way back through the bustle to where he saw Stewart standing.

One of the matchmaking mamas Stewart had warned him about interrupted his progress. "Ah, dear Lieutenant Redding!" she said. "How nice it is to see you again!"

Bollocks. He recognized the older woman who somehow believed that if a little bit of gold was good, more must be better. Her entire dress was gold, and she was outfitted with gold earrings, gold bracelets, a gold necklace and even a gold turban. She looked like she belonged in an Egyptian temple.

Jonathan strained his brain, but had no idea who she was. A countess? A duchess? A missus? Oh, dear. He grabbed for her hand and bowed low over it, brushing a kiss across her gold-gloved knuckle. "It is indeed my pleasure to see you again," he said, hoping that his charm would distract her from his lack of use of her title and proper introduction. "And who is with you, pray tell?"

"Oh, you remember my daughter, Lady Sarah?" the mama said, moving slightly to reveal a girl behind her, and lightly hitting Jonathan with her fan. Jonathan fought the urge to wince when it hit him, and instead bowed low over the young girl's hand as well. She was wearing white, and her countenance was about as pale as her dress. Her large brown eyes looked like saucers on her face, giving her the impression of a wide-eyed ghost. "Of course," Jonathan murmured. "And how are you enjoying the ball?" he asked the girl.

"Um... I... er... very well, m'lord."

Jonathan gave a slight chuckle. "Just Lieutenant," he told her with a wink and released her hand.

"How have you been enjoying the Season, Lieutenant?" the gold monstrosity asked him. Jonathan hated the small talk of balls- hundreds of people saying nothing, all at the same time. There was an art to it, he knew, but he found it terribly tedious and boring. How was the weather? It was England- it was rainy. End of discussion.

"I was going to ask you the same thing," Jonathan said, turning the conversation back to the woman. She seemed a talkative sort. "But perhaps I could escort you both over to the refreshment table while you tell me what amusements have kept you occupied lately?" He offered one arm to the mama, and then his other to the young debutante, who looked like she was going to faint. Perhaps some food would help her, he thought.

It took several minutes, but Jonathan managed to extricate himself from his gold accoutrement when another group of young misses walked up. He knew it was probably to talk to him, but it was convenient enough to merely bow over the girl in white's hand and leave. "Lady Sarah," he said, taking her hand again and bowing low, then giving a slight deferential nod to her mother and the gaggle of girls who surrounded them. "Ladies," he said, again figuring that the mama would be more focused on the attention he paid to her daughter than again neglecting to address her title. The girls started tittering after he left and he had to laugh. Oh, it was cruel to play with them like that, but he figured he had risen Sarah's popularity tenfold, and that would eventually lead out to a more promising marriage. It was like playing chess, Jonathan thought, but with real people.

"Ah, Jonathan!" Stewart said when he spied Jonathan across the room, heading towards him. "We were wondering where you were." He motioned with his hand for Jonathan to come join him.

Jonathan's breath caught, and he felt his heart jump. It often did that when he saw Stewart. *Damn man doesn't know how handsome he is.*

"Good evening Stewart. Good evening... my lords," Jonathan said, addressing the three other men standing next to Stewart. They were probably all titled. He couldn't remember.

"Jonathan," Stewart said, pulling Jonathan to his side to include him into the conversation, "we were just discussing whether or not one must dance in order to remain in polite society."

Jonathan wanted to kiss Stewart for pulling him close (hell, he just wanted to kiss Stewart), but at the same time he felt like hitting him for drawing him into such a conversation. "I'm sure the gentlemen can appreciate that your injury prevents you from dancing," he said diplomatically.

"But then how would one know which woman to choose as his wife, if not to touch her, see how graceful she moves?" one of the three nameless lords asked.

"I might suggest having a conversation with her," Jonathan said, grabbing a glass of champagne from a passing waiter.

"Would that not be a bit tedious?" asked another nameless lord. "What if she were terribly boring? At least when you're dancing you are otherwise entertained."

Jonathan hated this conversation. He knew why Stewart brought it up- most likely as revenge for his dictionary comment. "I notice that you gentlemen are not dancing," he said pointedly.

"We just came in from the card room," one of them said. Jonathan racked his brain to try to remember which one was not speaking, but failed. Really, how was he supposed to keep track of who they were? They were even dressed alike.

"Lieutenant Redding, will you be going out for the next set?" one of the men said. How the hell did they know his name and he could not remember any one of theirs? Jonathan decided he would call them Git One, Git Two and Git Three.

"I am afraid I do not know how to dance," Jonathan admitted, swallowing the rest of his champagne and pawning the glass off on a passing servant, trying to ignore the embarrassment that was associated with that statement. "It comes from growing up the son of a poor vicar."

"Did they not teach you how to dance in the military?" asked an astonished Git Two, motioning to a few of the officers who were on the dance floor.

Jonathan narrowed his eyes at Stewart, who was now smiling innocently over his glass. "Yes," Jonathan admitted through gritted teeth, "For the officers. Alas, I went in as a regular. They really focus more on encouraging us to use our guns than our social skills."

"But you are a Lieutenant," said Git One. Or was it Git Three? Oh, bother.

"Last I checked," Jonathan said, making a show of looking at his uniform. "Why, yes, yes I am."

"I do not understand," Said Git Two, shaking his head.

Jonathan sighed and stared pointedly at Stewart, who was purposely looking another way. "I was not made an officer until almost the end of the war."

"Really? A decorated war hero as yourself?" said Git One. "Didn't you save this worthless muppet?" He nudged Stewart slightly, who merely smiled, and other two gits laughed.

Jonathan felt the anger rush through him so fast he became dizzy, and he took a deep breath. He knew the git was attempting at humor, and Stewart did not seem put out at all by his comment. Still, Jonathan was not getting into his history with these unnamed bastards. "Apparently," he said dismissively and decided a change of subject was in order. "But what about you three? Any young debutantes you see who strike your fancy?"

The men began to drone on about the young ladies, and who had the largest dowry, and who was declared an original or a diamond of the first water. Jonathan did not hear much of any of the conversation, allowing the voices of the young men to wash over him until they dismissed themselves to find young dance partners for their own.

"I hate it when you do that," Jonathan muttered after the gits had left.

"Turnabout," Stewart smiled, "is fair play."

"Still," Jonathan said, "I hate having to bring up my background. It makes me feel... less, somehow."

"You have every right to be here as they do," admonished Stewart. "The invitation was addressed to you as well."

"Do you really think that I would receive an invitation if I did not reside in your house?" Jonathan challenged.

"Yes," Stewart said simply. "Lord Talbot was correct; you are a decorated war hero. And truly, Jonathan, you *should* learn how to dance."

Jonathan scowled and turned back to watch the dancers. So Git One was Lord Talbot. "Then who would keep you company?" he asked.

Stewart smiled and patted Jonathan on the back. "True enough," he said. "Let us find somewhere to sit. I fear the cold is paining my knee."

Cold? It was terribly warm in there. Jonathan did not argue, but guided Stewart to the card room to an empty table. "Perhaps I can find a server who has something stronger than champagne," Jonathan said. "I'll go see." Stewart just grunted his approval and settled himself into a chair.

Jonathan flagged down a passing server, who promised to bring him a brandy. The flurry of dresses and coats through the doorway caught Jonathan's eye and he felt his heart grip sadly. He would love to be on the dance floor. He would love to learn to waltz. But what was the point, if he could not dance with Stewart?

CHAPTER FIFTEEN

"Died from heat exhaustion," in the middle of the London spring
Season seemed ironic, but Jonathan was more than happy to exit the
stifling heat of the ballroom and step into their carriage to go home.
Jonathan sighed contentedly as he sank into the coach, pulling off his
gloves and hat. Stewart had taken the rear facing seat. "I swear I'm
amazed we got out of there without finding ourselves engaged,"
Jonathan said.

"I believe the number of debutantes grows each year," Stewart
agreed, settling in, standing his cane in front of him and resting his
hands on it.

"They are little more than children. I am always surprised that they
are married off so young." Jonathan thought of his own sister; at 17,
she was ready for her own Season.

Stewart shrugged. "It is the way of things, I suppose."

"I cannot imagine being married at 18. Why, I was already 20 when
I met you."

"Nowhere near marrying material at that age, I agree."

Jonathan made a face at Stewart before leaning back against the seat
and closing his eyes, enjoying the slight sway of the carriage. He did
not remember feeling so fatigued after a ball before. He must be getting
old.

"Would you like children?" Stewart asked.

Jonathan felt the edges of his mouth quirk up. "I believe I can safely
say that having children is not in my future." He paused, then added,
"Why? Are you secretly engaged?"

Stewart did not reply, but remained quiet, and a horrible thought
rushed through Jonathan's brain. He pushed his head back from the
squabs. "Stewart?" Are you thinking of getting married? Having
children?" No, say no. He knew that it was not as if he and Stewart
had any real future; although Stewart was not directly in line for the
dukedom, he was an Earl, and as such he would be expected to marry
and beget an heir. After the past five years of living together in
England, Jonathan had lured himself into a sense of contentment with
his life with Stewart, and had even engaged in fantasies- well, in

addition to *those* fantasies- wherein he and Stewart would grow old together. To think that that dream was over... Jonathan's heart ached at the thought, and he rubbed his chest absentmindedly.

Stewart remained silent, merely continued resting his hands on his cane, staring out the window. Jonathan felt his heart constrict. He had fifteen wonderful years with Stewart; that was enough, right? It wasn't as if his heart would actually break apart. Probably.

"Died of a broken heart." How droll.

"Stewart?" Jonathan said after several minutes went by. "Stew- talk to me. I won't be angry. I can move out when you marry. I can still work as your secretary- or not, if you choose. Just please, talk to me." Jonathan reached across the seat and rested his hand on Stewart's good knee, squeezing it gently, to try to get Stewart's attention.

Stewart looked back at Jonathan. "When have I ever mentioned getting married, Jonathan?"

"Never, but with the talk in the ball, and then your questions now..." Jonathan trailed off, trying to read Stewart's eyes in the passing lamplight, which was difficult to impossible.

Stewart patted the hand that Jonathan still had on his knee a few times, finally resting his hand on there, and absentmindedly began rubbing small circles with his thumb. He turned to stare out the window again.

Jonathan was certain his hand was going to catch fire. From the moment that Stewart rested his hand upon his, his heart caught in his chest and squeezed painfully. When Stewart began his lazy circles across the back of his hand, he was fairly certain his heart blew apart in his chest. Trying to keep deep, even breaths, afraid that any sudden movement would break the contact, Jonathan submitted to Stewart's ignorant torture. The electricity that seemed to course through his veins whenever Stewart touched him had not waivered since they had first met, and tonight was no different.

"I was thinking of a starting a school," Stewart's deep voice finally broke the silence.

"A school?" Jonathan squeaked.

Stewart smiled and turned back to face Jonathan, cocking his head to the side. "Yes, what do you think?"

"A school? For boys, I assume? Or girls? Or both?"

Stewart shrugged. "I hadn't thought about it, actually, but probably for boys. Those from the lower classes, who may not be able to afford such schooling without a patron to support them."

As I had, Jonathan thought, and smiled. "Stewart! That's wonderful! What are you going to call it? The Lennox School for Boys. No, the Lennox Lyceum; the alliteration is better. Where are you thinking of having it? And the curriculum? Will the school be a boarding school, or a day school or both?" Jonathan paused, realizing that he was the only one speaking, and that Stewart was staring at him.

"Oh, that's what you were talking to your brother about tonight, yes? But then you probably don't need my help," Jonathan said, and with that he drew his hand back and sat as far back into the buttery leather seat as possible. Perhaps it could swallow him whole. "Death by leather seat." That sounded like a new penny dreadful novel. "I apologize, you know how I get sometimes." Jonathan faked a laugh. "I'll just uh... you just let me know if you need any help."

Several more minutes went by, which felt like hours. Or days. Devil take it, how big was London, anyway? Shouldn't they have gotten to their house by now?

"I told the driver to take the long way," Stewart said, breaking the silence.

Jonathan groaned. "Did I just speak my thoughts aloud again?"

Shaking his head, a small smile graced Stewart's visage. "No, dear friend. I have known you a long time. Sometimes I believe I can read your thoughts."

Read his thoughts? No, no, no. That would be horrible. Then Stewart would know about how he felt, and he definitely would no longer want Jonathan living with him, or even working with him. That could never, never happen. "That's deuced uncomfortable," Jonathan said, finally.

"Why?" Stewart laughed. "You think you cannot do it as well? What am I thinking now?"

Jonathan narrowed his eyes. "You are thinking you are having a great deal of fun at my expense."

"See? I told you," Stewart said, looking back out the window, and falling silent again.

Several moments passed before Jonathan broke the silence. "You are concerned you are failing your father and his legacy," Jonathan said quietly.

"Yes," Stewart whispered, closing his eyes.

"Do you want to?"

"What? Get married? Beget heirs?" Stewart laughed sarcastically and leveling a look at Jonathan.

"Have children," Jonathan asked evenly. "You never answered my question."

"Honestly? I don't know." Stewart shook his head. "I believe I am selfish, Jonathan. I do not wish my life to change one bit. I am perfectly content to live the rest of my life in this manner."

He should stop now, while he was ahead. He should take that statement for what it was, and not push further. His obstinate self, however, refused to comply. "But?" Jonathan prodded.

Stewart sighed. "But... but if I get married and have children, will I be happier than I am now? I cannot imagine that. Would I be a good father? I would hope, but I keep wondering if I cannot merely be a good role model to my nephews and perhaps those who attend the school instead. The more sons my brother has, the farther I get from having to inherit the Dukedom, so I need not bother concerning myself with that. I'm what... fourth or fifth in line now? Nowhere near fearing to take over that outrageous task. My title is a courtesy one, and will pass to my nephew upon my death if I don't have children. Still, I fear that I am irresponsible to keep bringing up my own desires first, and marriage and children second."

Jonathan's heart flip-flopped at this announcement, but he knew the decision was far from over. Jonathan rubbed his chest again. He did not want to ask the question, but he did, anyway. "Are there any women you've met that you fancy marrying, and, er... begetting these heirs with?"

Stewart barked a laugh. "You have the most interesting way of putting things, Jonathan. I swear it seems you are constantly filtering your thoughts with me."

You would not be anywhere near me if I did not. "You didn't answer my question."

Stewart shook his head. "No, and not for lack of looking. Many are lovely women." *Ouch*, thought Jonathan. That hurt his heart. It shouldn't hurt, but it did. Pain shot through to his left arm, and he began rubbing that, instead.

"Did you find anyone particularly intriguing tonight?" Stewart asked.

You. "What? No!" barked Jonathan, a little too quickly.

Stewart laughed. "I saw you with a group of young ladies," he said. "They seemed quite taken with you."

"I would never…" Jonathan started, then mentally checked himself. "I would never be attracted to someone the same age as my…" he paused again. "That young. Right. They were too young." He panted the last part out.

"They were at that," Stewart said absentmindedly.

"But..." Jonathan prodded again, trying not to focus on the stabbing sensation. Had it always been this warm in the carriage? He tugged at his cravat, pulling it away from his neck.

"You will find me odd for saying this," Stewart said.

"I promise you that even if I do, I will tell you I do not."

"Terribly unhelpful of you," Stewart sighed. "I just... when I think of my life as an old man, in fifty years, I think of you and I sitting over a chessboard, or arguing about how close to sit near the fire. I don't see a woman or children in that vision."

"Does that... bother you?" Jonathan was fairly certain that his poor heart was about to give out, the number of times it had been surprised in the past hour. "Died of shock," seemed a bit prosaic, however.

"Bother me... what? No, no, I tell you that's why I believe I am selfish. I am quite content." He paused for a moment. "Except for Parliament. Parliament is awful," he scowled.

Jonathan smiled. "Then it is good that your brother has taken up his duty in regards to his seat in the House, then, yes?"

"True," Stewart said, pondering for a moment. "Then perfectly content, yes. I cannot think of one thing I would change."

Jonathan could think of a few things, but that would definitely end their lovely camaraderie. "So... what do you think of Lennox Lyceum?" he offered again, breaking the silence.

"Bloody terrible," Stewart laughed.

Jonathan chuckled along with him, and moved his hand across his cravat again, taking a large breath. With fumbling hands, he loosened the white strip of cloth and took it off completely, feeling the cool air against his neck. He sat back against the squabs again, trying not to breathe too heavily. His heart ached, most likely from their conversation, and he rubbed his chest again. Glancing over, Stewart smiled. "Tied your cravat too tightly again, eh, Jonathan? Perhaps we should get *you* a valet."

Jonathan did his best to smile at Stewart. "Yes," he managed, now pulling at his shirt. He felt confined by his clothing. Damn and blast, why did the new styles have coats so tightly fitting? He could barely move, and the sleeves were cutting off circulation to his left arm. And why was it so warm? As the horses continued trotting, and Stewart continued to stare out the window, Jonathan felt himself break out in a cold sweat. His heart was pounding, pounding so loudly he could not hear anything for the pounding. Would the carriage never reach their house? And why, why did his entire body suddenly seem to hurt? Jonathan closed his eyes, trying to will away the pain, and counted the seconds until the damn carriage would stop.

On the opposite side of the carriage Stewart counted the streetlights as they neared the townhouse. He enjoyed the various entertainments of London, even though he knew Jonathan would just as soon stay at home as go out. It was good for Jonathan, he thought, to talk with others, if for nothing else to remind the pompous haute ton that intelligence had nothing to do with birthright. The school Stewart had been imagining would also be a blight on the ton- educating the lower classes as if they were lords? How gauche. He smiled at the thought. Perhaps he and Jonathan could visit the solicitor tomorrow and start looking for a place to house the school. Boarding and a day school option? He had not considered that. Thank God for Jonathan and his forward-thinking.

"Jonathan, I was thinking," Stewart said, turning his head back to his friend. "Good God! Jonathan!" he yelled, scrambling across the carriage seat. Jonathan was slumped up against the corner of the seat, breathing heavily and, Stewart realized upon closer examination, bathed in sweat. "Jonathan! Jonathan! Wake up, man!" he said, lightly shaking Jonathan's shoulder. At that moment, the carriage stopped and lurched forward. Stewart fell back against the seat, then pushed himself back up and fumbled against the door, to a very surprised footman. "Help me!" Stewart pleaded. "Come! Grab him!" The footman, after recovering for a moment, reached in and pulled Jonathan out by his shoulders. Stewart held his legs, trying to keep his balance on his bad leg, slipping as he exited the carriage.

"I've got him, my lord," Stewart heard another footman say, and Jonathan's weight was released from him. Stewart stumbled forward, catching himself on his good leg, and turned around. "Henry! Henry!" he called to his driver. "Fetch Dr. Lambrose! Quickly!" He turned around and rushed as quickly as he was able into the waiting house as the carriage took off.

Within a few minutes, the inside of the house was a panic; servants were scurrying to and fro, most likely just having been awakened by the ruckus. Stewart ignored them and hobbled up the stairs where the footmen were laying Jonathan down on the bed.

Stewart rushed in, shooing the footmen away. "Go! Look for the doctor, and send him up at once!" he yelled, not noticing their replies. Roberts appeared at the doorway as the footmen exited. "May I be of service, my lord?" he asked Stewart, wringing his hands.

"Roberts!" Stewart looked up. "Yes! Help me... help me remove his jacket and shirt." With much difficulty, they removed Jonathan's jacket and waistcoat from his unmoving body, but Stewart was harkened with the knowledge that Jonathan was still breathing, albeit shallowly.

"Stewart?" Jonathan asked weakly when he was stripped of everything but his shirt and breeches.

"Jonathan! Thank God!" Stewart all but cried as he laid Jonathan down on the bed. "The doctor will be here soon."

"What happened?" Jonathan asked weakly.

"Don't talk," Stewart ordered.

"So tired," Jonathan murmured. "Must be... getting old."

Stewart took in a shaky breath as he watched his friend's pale chest take shallow breaths as he lay against the pillows. He had seen countless young men in the throes of death in battle, but Jonathan was not one of those countless young men he had commanded. He was, well... he was *Jonathan.*

Roberts spoke up, pulling Stewart out of his trance. "I believe Dr. Lambrose has arrived," he said, and indeed a moment later the heavyset doctor came in, dressed in evening clothes.

"I was on my way back from a dinner party when your driver accosted me," the doctor said sarcastically. "Luckily I am used to lords needing help at all hours of the night, and had my bag with me. Now, how may I be of service?"

"Doctor!" Stewart said, ignoring him, "thank God you're here. He just... he collapsed in the carriage. He woke momentarily, but I told him not to speak."

"Very good," Dr. Lambrose said, his sarcastic tone evaporating upon realizing there was a true emergency. He walked quickly across the room towards Jonathan. "Any history of fainting spells?" he asked, picking up Jonathan's hand and feeling his pulse.

"Um... no."

"Has this happened before?"

"No, never. He's always been in the best of health. Rarely even gets a sniffle," Stewart said.

"Hello, Doctor," Jonathan mumbled quietly, one eye slitting open before closing again. "You didn't have to dress so formally just to see me, you know."

Dr. Lambrose frowned at Jonathan, putting his hand gently back down. He then turned his gaze to Stewart. "I see. Well, I am going to examine the patient, so if you would be so kind to step out..." he waved to the door with his hand.

"Um... of course," Stewart said, moving to the door and stepping outside. He took a shaky breath as he leaned up against the wall. He would have paced up the hallway, but his knee was paining him something awful. He should go downstairs and put it up, but he remained rooted to his spot; there was no way he was going to leave until he knew that Jonathan would live. Rubbing his face with his hands, he felt his stubble that was already beginning to grow in.

Jonathan would not be able to shave him tomorrow, he thought, wondering at once where that idea had come from. If Jonathan died... Stewart felt his heart drop like lead. Jonathan could not die- that was the simple fact. He was an Earl, by God, and a retired Colonel. If Doctor Lambrose could not help him, he would find someone who could.

Several minutes later, Dr. Lambrose came out of the room, pulling the door closed behind him.

"So?" asked Stewart. "Is he going to be all right? What happened?"

"Angina Pectoris, I would imagine," Dr. Lambrose said gravely.

"Angina?"

"Angina Pectoris," the doctor corrected, "although currently there does not seem to be a cardiac insufficiency."

"Cardiac... so it's his heart?" Stewart felt his own heart grip tighter in his chest. Perhaps he was suffering from the same affliction.

"Did he complain about any shortness of breath, tiredness, pain in his chest or left arm?"

"Well, yes... he said he felt... odd this morning, but did not seem to be ill otherwise. I... I made him go out tonight. He said he was having trouble breathing in the carriage on the way home... one moment he was fine, and when I turned around he was unconscious. Did... Do you think the shock of going out was the cause?" Stewart felt his heart stop beating for a moment and he stared at a spot just over Dr. Lambrose's shoulder. What if Jonathan had died? What if this was his fault?

"Most likely not," Dr. Lambrose assured him, putting his hand on Stewart's shoulder and shaking him a bit to bring him out of shock. "If he had been complaining about symptoms as early as this morning, he was most likely already starting the attack. At this point he is alive and awake," Stewart felt the ground underneath him sway, "but it is very important that he is kept relaxed and has no stress for several days. I will leave some medicine and a list of acceptable foods with the housekeeper, but most importantly, he needs to eat and sleep regularly."

"That will not be a problem, Doctor. I can ensure you he will." He would set a clock if he had to.

"And no stress."

"Not a problem." No paper, no visitors, no servant issues.

"And no drinking," Dr. Lambrose said, huffing out his chest.

"That might be a problem," Stewart mumbled. "I will... I will make sure that is not a problem, Doctor," he promised, noting Dr. Lambrose's intense gaze.

"He was lucky this time, Lord Durnley, but I cannot guarantee he will be again. If he has a severe attack, there will not be anything I can do for him. At this point, his health is in his hands... and yours," he added.

"Of course, Dr. Lambrose."

"One more thing, if I may?" the doctor lowered his voice and stepped farther into the hallway. Surprised, Stewart stepped in closer to hear the doctor.

"What is it, Doctor?"

"I noticed... well, I noticed upon just a cursory examination that Lieutenant Redding appears to be an affable chap."

"Yes, he usually is," Stewart agreed.

Dr. Lambrose narrowed his eyes. "Don't you think that's odd, given that he almost died this evening?" he questioned.

"Yes, well... Jonathan... Lieutenant Redding doesn't often give in to emotional tirades. To be honest, I rarely see him get overly angry or excited about anything."

"That's exactly what I mean," Dr. Lambrose said. "I see this more often with patients who suffer from dyspepsia or gastritis, but sometimes it does manifest itself in heart issues."

Stewart's eyes narrowed. "What are you saying, Doctor?"

"I'm saying that if he continues to keep up the facade that there is never anything amiss, he will continue to put stress onto his heart, and it will give out again, and more frequently. Possibly... permanently."

Stewart felt all of the air go out of his lungs. "I see," he said.

"I am not certain if there is anything you can do, but I think he would take such news better from you than he would me."

"Yes," Stewart said absently. He blinked, trying to get his bearings. "I... uh, I appreciate your coming so quickly. Roberts can settle up with you, and Henry can see you get to wherever you need to go."

"Yes, yes, well, it is rather late, so home it is. Good evening, Lord Durnley."

"Yes, good evening, Doctor," Stewart said automatically as the doctor walked down the hall. He took a bracing breath before entering Jonathan's bedroom.

He realized as he entered that he had rarely been in Jonathan's bedroom- usually Jonathan was attending to him in his. It was decorated much as he remembered it, although there were a few changes- the painting they had bought from an artist selling his wares on the sidewalk last year hung on the far wall, an overstuffed leather chair covered with various clothes was sitting near the fireplace, a throw pillow had fallen on the ground next to a large stack of books and an equally tall stack of papers- they all seemed to make it more... more... Jonathan somehow. Stewart walked towards the fire and braced a hand on the mantle.

"I feel deuced embarrassed, you know," Jonathan said from the bed. Stewart glanced over at his large frame under the thin coverlet. The sheet was pulled up to his waist, his chest bare from the doctor's examination. Stewart glanced to the jacket and shirt, still lying haphazardly on the ground.

Stewart bent to pick them up and placed them across the chair with the other clothing, his tongue lodged somewhere in his throat. Seeing Jonathan lying there, pale as the sheet he had pulled up against him, left him with a myriad of emotions. He stared at the fire for several moments, trying to collect himself, his eyes closed. "If you didn't really want to go to the ball, Jonathan, you know you could have just said no," he sputtered, trying for humor.

"I'm sorry, Stewart," Jonathan said from the bed.

"*You're sorry*?" Stewart spun around. "Whatever for?"

"For upsetting you," he said.

Stewart crossed to the other side of the room and stood over Jonathan, no, *towered* over Jonathan. "Now look here... you... you..." he stared into Jonathan's eyes and was surprised not only to see pain, but also sadness. A deep sadness, he noted. It made him want to weep.

Dear God, he was getting maudlin. That was understandable- his friend had almost died. But getting emotional now was not going to help.

"I... what?" Jonathan asked softly.

Stewart sighed and sat heavily on the bed, realizing once he was sitting just how much his knee had been paining him. "I do not know what I would do if you had died," he said simply, and reached over haphazardly, putting his own hand over Jonathan's and squeezing.

"Indeed, who would make sure your eggs were boiled just right? Or your cravats were tied just so?" Jonathan said half-jokingly, his eyes immediately watering.

Stewart shook his head. "That's not what I meant, and you know it. But this is not the time. I wanted to let you know that the doctor has left you instructions so this does not happen again."

Jonathan blinked several times as if to assimilate the information and narrowed his eyes. "What type of list?"

"Foods you should and should not eat, I suppose. But mostly that you are supposed to rest and eat regularly."

Jonathan sighed deeply. "Seems simple enough."

"And no working," Stewart said quickly.

Jonathan's eyes furrowed. "No working?"

"No. No, no," Stewart said, taking his hand from Jonathan's and holding it up. "You have not taken a vacation in, what... five years? It is high time you did so."

Fifteen. "I don't have anywhere I want to go," he grumbled. *I don't want to leave you.*

"That is too bloody bad," Stewart said angrily, "for we are leaving for the country estate the day after tomorrow." The words were out his mouth before could stop them, but yes, that was the ideal solution! Jonathan would have no choice but to rest while sequestered out in the country, and he could keep a closer eye on him there.

"But it's the middle of the Season!" Jason said, sitting upright.

Stewart placed his hand on Jonathan's chest and pushed him back down. Jonathan's breath quickened, but he complied and rested back against the pillows. "You and I both know you could care less about the Season, and I find that I care more about your health than I do a few balls or the opera," Stewart insisted. "Besides," he said, his voice softening, "you can help me plan the school."

Jonathan's eyes softened. *He cares more about me than the Season. That had to mean something, right?* "That would mean working, you know," he smiled.

"We will see. But I did not tell you the best part about the school while we were in the carriage. I am quite despondent that I neglected to do so; I believe you would have foregone your histrionics if I had."

"Most likely. I believe this entire episode began when you told me my idea for a name was, what? 'Bloody terrible' if I recall."

"And it was. 'Lennox Lyceum.'" Stewart scoffed, "It's not the Duke's school, anyway, or my brother's."

"Your brother is the Duke."

"In my mind my father will always be the Duke," Stewart said. "But that's not the point. The point is that the school is mine. And I shall call it whatever I choose."

"Of course, your highness... I mean, my lord," Jonathan said, rolling his eyes.

"That's Colonel to you, Lieutenant," Stewart said haughtily.

"Of course, Colonel Ainsley. At your service," Jonathan laughed giving a mock salute.

Stewart laughed. "You have not changed from that first evening when I met you."

"You mean when I single-handedly led the charge that took out two dozen French cannons, leading the way for our cavalry to overtake a strategic battle site? You mean that evening? Apparently I am quite the war hero, you know."

"Yes, that evening," Stewart said, choosing to ignore the "hero" comment, "when you somehow coerced me into calling you by your first name, feeding you, and then plying you with so much liquor you were ill for two days."

"Coerced you? I did no such thing. You only did so because you wanted to."

Stewart's eyebrows shot up. "*I* wanted to?"

"Yes," Jonathan said, looking away while he smoothed the sheet in front of him. "I merely... encouraged your desires."

Stewart smiled. "Now I know you're off your head," he said.

A sliver of fear sliced through Jonathan at Stewart's insinuation, and his heart beat quickly and a spasm gripped him. Instinctively, he grabbed at his chest and groaned.

"What? Are you having another attack?" Stewart said in a panicked voice. "I can get the doctor back if necessary."

Jonathan took a deep breath, and the pain subsided, but he kept his eyes closed. "I'm all right," he groaned. "Probably like... the doctor said. Too much... excitement." He tried to laugh, but it came out more like a moan.

Stewart swallowed the lump that had crept into his throat. He picked up Jonathan's hand and cradled it to his chest. "Jonathan, I promise you, I will take care of you as you did me."

"No... need," Jonathan breathed. "I'll be right as rain tomorrow, just you see."

"And then we're leaving for the country."

"Let's talk about it tomorrow," Jonathan said in a strained voice. "Sometimes earls don't always get their way, you know," he smiled under hooded eyes.

"That reminds me," Stewart said, gently placing Jonathan's hand back at his side. "The doctor had one more bit of instruction."

"What might that be? Not bleeding, I hope."

"Worse," Stewart grimaced.

"Worse than bleeding?" Jonathan asked, his eyes blinking open. "What is it?"

"No alcohol."

"What? Bloody hell!" Jonathan yelled.

CHAPTER SIXTEEN

"Sobriety killed him," seemed something more along the line of John Wesley's tombstone, but Jonathan was fairly certain he could qualify as well. Damn Stewart, who had locked up every single bottle of wine and liquor in the wine cellar below, taking the keys from both Roberts and Mrs. Banks. He had hidden them somewhere, and Jonathan was fairly certain it would be easier to study the art of lock picking than in trying to find out where Stewart had sequestered them.

And dammit all to hell, he was *bored*.

Stewart hadn't just locked up the liquor, he had also banned the paper (all of them, even the gossip sheets), given orders to Roberts that they were not receiving visitors, and locked the door to Jonathan's study, promising only that he would relinquish the key when Dr. Lambrose gave his approval. Jonathan paced the library for probably the fiftieth time that morning; while he enjoyed reading, he was not one to sit around and do nothing, not unless he was in the grips of melancholia. He feared that if he did not distract his mind soon, that was exactly what would happen.

And then what would Stewart say, if he saw him like that? Probably commit him to a mental institution as the vicar had his mother.

Speaking of the vicar, what was the date? If Stewart would just allow the paper, he could check that, but no, he did not even know what the goddamned day was! Jonathan stopped himself from pacing and took a breath. Stewart was just trying to take care of him in his overbearing, heavy-handed way. He supposed he should at least give him credit for trying.

Jonathan thought back. When was the evening of his attack? The ball was the... 17th? 20th? Somewhere around there... the days all merged together for him during the Season with its fripperies and entertainments. He had lost a few days languishing in bed, but he surmised that it was close to the end of the month, if not the last day. Susanna would be looking for his monthly letter and bank note (mostly bank note, he assumed). He moved to the desk and drew out a thick sheet of paper. Memories of clerking for the vicar suddenly came to mind, when he would labor painstakingly over the thinnest pieces of paper, trying to use as much of the small, inexpensive sheet as possible while still keeping his hand legible. Nothing like being an Earl- or working for an Earl- to forget such habits. His written hand now was much larger and flowing.

Dearest Susanna, he wrote, *I hope this letter finds you well. Enclosed is the usual amount, and please remember not to tell the vicar, or else he will make you tithe half of it. Or all of it, if he knows it is from me. I have not heard from your sisters, but I assume that they are doing well and are enjoying their respective confinements. You would think that they would have ample enough time to write their poor, lonely brother, and you may tell them I said as much. As for me,* Jonathan stopped writing. Did he tell her about his attack? Would it worry her unnecessarily? *As for me, I have been ill for the past week, but now feel fit as a fiddle, and am eager to get back to the enjoyments of the Season.* Jonathan scoffed at his own words. He hated the Season, but how to explain why he put himself through such torture, except to be with the man he loved, who did not know he was the object of such affection? It was all so very convoluted. *Stewart ensures that we are seen at the theatre or opera at least once a week, and I have been to so many balls I can honestly say I cannot remember them all. Next year, dear sister, if you wish, you may have your Season and I will be proud to introduce you. Stewart has a sister as well, and I am certain she would be willing to sponsor you.*

Until your next installment, I remain,
Your Brother
p.s. Make sure not to spend it all on hair ribbons this time!

Jonathan smiled at his post script. That would annoy Susanna to no end- she was rarely spending money on such things, although his two other sisters had no issue doing so when he had sent money to them. Now they had husbands, however, and Jonathan figured he no longer had to support their ribbon habit. Susanna, however, would probably spend the money on the upkeep on the rectory that the benefactor did not bother to maintain, nor would the vicar bother to ask, as he was busy writing some sermon damning one group or another to hell. He felt anger at his father rush through his veins, but soothed it just as quickly; in one more year, Susanna would be free from the vicar, safely ensconced in London, and Jonathan's obligation- at least financially- would be complete. If the vicar wanted to subside in a run-down house alone, he had only himself to blame.

Jonathan stood, suddenly, thoughts of his father frustrating him. No, not his father, *the vicar.* He had thought of him solely as the vicar since his mother had been sent to the asylum for melancholia and had never returned. When it appeared that Jonathan was having similar issues, the vicar would beat him severely, telling him that he was giving him a reason for his wallowing. And so he became merely the vicar, as Jonathan could not fathom that a father would do such a thing to his wife or son.

Jonathan blotted his letter before folding the heavy paper gently. He placed it and a bank note in an envelope, not so much for the luxury, but as a physical warning to his sister that it was from him, and to be kept from the prying eyes of the vicar. Sealing the letter with his own wax seal that Stewart had allowed him to take from his study after much duress, he walked it to the entryway and placed it on the silver platter for outgoing mail.

Walking back into the library, Jonathan swore. He *was* going to suffer some type of mania if he did not do *something.* With another oath, he turned back around and grabbed the letter and his coat and hat and slipped out the door before a footman or Roberts caught him leaving. Certainly Stewart could not begrudge him a simple walk outside. Pulling his greatcoat closer to him to ward off the spring chill, Jonathan turned towards the direction of the post office and let loose a breath he had not realized he had been holding.

The fresh air helped. As fresh as it could get in London, anyway.

CHAPTER SEVENTEEN

"Death by wind," sounded odd, but "Blown to death," sounded naughty. Jonathan gripped his greatcoat more tightly around him as he battled the random storm that had come up only a few minutes after he had delivered his letter. It had taken him much longer to walk home than he had anticipated, and he was mourning his lack of gloves and scarf. More than that, he found himself afraid that Stewart would find out he had been walking in this weather. Guilt crept over him just as heavily as the chill that pervaded his bones. Damn, springtime in London was as cold as the winter.

By the time Jonathan found his way back to the townhome, he felt chilled inside and out. A nice, hot bath sounded like heaven, along with a lovely cup of tea. Preferably with brandy, but if it were hot, he would take it either way. Jonathan found himself daydreaming about bathing in tea when the front door opened.

"Master Redding!" Roberts said, holding the door open wide. "Lord Durnley has been turning the house upside down in search of you." He pulled off Jonathan's soaking jacket and took his hat as Jonathan stepped inside. Ruined, Jonathan thought dismally as he peered at what used to be his favorite hat. Now it was just a mass of wet, melted fabric.

"Yes, Roberts, I apologize. I thought just to slip out for a short walk and got caught in the storm. I should have told you where I was going."

"Yes, sir," Roberts agreed, "but we are glad you're back. I assume you would like a hot bath brought up to your room?"

"I do believe I will do my best to get Durnley to double your salary if you do," Jonathan smiled through chattering teeth.

"Excellent," Roberts said. "I'll send someone up now. Lord Durnley, last I checked, was in the library," Roberts hinted.

"Yes, Roberts, I'll go calm the raging beast," Jonathan sighed. "It's my fault, in any case."

"Very good, sir. If I may say, sir, it is only because he cares for your well-being."

"I know," Jonathan said. "Thank you, Roberts."

Roberts beamed at him before exiting. Most servants were not thanked for doing their job, but Jonathan had not been born into the life of privilege. It seemed foreign to him to just expect others to do things for them without even a social nicety.

Dripping across the marble entryway, Jonathan made his way to the library, where he saw Stewart staring out the large bay window. He cleared his throat loudly once, twice, and was reminded of the time when he first met Stewart, the arrogant Major who had made him stand for two hours at attention before he would acknowledge him. Jonathan was fairly certain he would be frozen to death by then. "Froze to death" seemed so common, somehow.

"I'm back," he said weakly, rubbing his arms for warmth.

Stewart did not turn around. "I heard you come in," he said, his voice hard.

"I just stepped out for a short walk," Jonathan explained, trying to keep his teeth from chattering. "I got caught in the rain on the way back." He looked down at the puddle he was dripping onto the floor.

"Dammit, Jonathan, you almost died last week. *Died.* Does that mean nothing to you? Because it sure as hell means something to me." Stewart turned around. "I knew- I just knew- we should have gone straight out to the country. I can't *believe* I allowed you to talk me into staying in London. I don't believe I am being overly- dear God, you're soaking wet." Stewart rushed across the library to where Jonathan was standing.

"Yes," Jonathan chattered. "I believe they have a bath upstairs waiting for when you are quite done chastising me."

"Done chastising you? You'll be old and grey by the time I'm done with that." He grabbed Jonathan by the shoulders and physically turned him around. "Come on, man, let's get you up to your bath before you catch your death."

"I really did only intend to go out for a short walk," Jonathan insisted as Stewart guided him up the stairs.

"I believe you," Stewart sighed. "Did you at least take a coat and a hat?"

"Yes," Jonathan said like a petulant schoolboy. "But... I forgot... my gloves," he said, his chattering getting worse.

"You forgot your- of course you did. And you didn't think to hail a hackney to get home, I suppose?"

"It... was a short... walk."

"I swear, Jonathan, what would you do without me?"

"The... same as... you would me," Jonathan said. "Wither away... and die... I suppose." He tried for a smile but it came out more like a grimace.

Stewart gave a long suffering sigh. "I would argue with you but I find I cannot." They turned the corner to Jonathan's room where a tub had just been filled. A footman stood with a bucket of hot water.

"Shoo," Stewart said, waving his hand at the footman. "We'll call if we need any more." The man glanced at Jonathan's dripping wet form in surprise before he stammered, "Yes, m'lord," and scurried out of the room.

"It... isn't nice... to shoo your... footman," Jonathan chattered.

"Stop talking," Stewart ordered. "I don't like hearing your teeth chattering."

Jonathan closed his mouth and began working at the stays on his cuffs, but his hands were shaking too badly. He looked fondly over at the water and debated just getting in fully clothed.

"Oh, stop," Stewart said, annoyed, pulling Jonathan's hands to the side. "Let me do it." With an efficiency that startled Jonathan, Stewart had his coat and shirt off within a few moments. "Boots," Stewart ordered, and Jonathan lifted first one leg, then the other, his hands around his midsection, shivering as Stewart pulled off his Hessians. Jonathan closed his eyes, wishing he could savor the moment of Stewart undressing him, but the cold and his shivering took any sort of sensual feeling out of the experience.

As he pulled off the second boot, Jonathan stepped down with his other foot for balance, exposing his back, which was a myriad of crisscrossed scars. "Bollocks!" Stewart exclaimed under his breath.

"What?" Jonathan asked, looking around. The bath looked quite inviting... perhaps he should just walk in with his breeches on.

"No, wait," Stewart said, as if he could read his mind. "Let me take those off." He knelt and untied Jonathan's breeches before pulling his socks and breeches down. "Go," he demanded waving off a fully naked Jonathan, who walked dutifully to the bath and sank down in it.

The hot water was heavenly. "Died of bliss after a hot bath." There were certainly worse ways to go. Jonathan rested his head back and closed his eyes on a long sigh.

"Feeling better?" Stewart asked after several minutes.

Jonathan nodded. He had almost forgotten Stewart was behind him. His smile quirked up at the sides. "Did you want to join me?" he joked.

"It does look inviting," Stewart said.

Jonathan jerked around in surprise, but lost his balance and slipped down, his head going under the water. He pushed himself up, gasping for breath, to Stewart's laughter.

"Serves you right," Stewart admonished, "for making me worry all this afternoon."

"I said I was sorry," Jonathan grumbled, rubbing water from his eyes.

"So you did," Stewart agreed. He handed Jonathan the soap. "I assume you can do that by yourself," he said.

Jonathan nodded, and suddenly realized his state of nakedness. *Lord, I'm naked in front of Stewart.*

"I'll... just go," Stewart said awkwardly. "Do you need me to lay your clothes out before I go?"

Jonathan barked a laugh. "You wouldn't know where to begin."

Stewart narrowed his eyes, prepared to be offended, but then shrugged. "You're right," he said. "I'll leave you to it." After a brief pause he stepped out of the room and closed the door.

Jonathan slid down into the heavenly warmth of the bath and sighed. He should feel guilty for making Stewart worry, but somehow all he could do was think about how concerned Stewart looked, and how he attended him. Jonathan smiled contentedly and closed his eyes, happy to be home.

CHAPTER EIGHTEEN

"His brain leaked out of his head," was quite graphic, but that is exactly what Jonathan supposed was happening. After his short walk in the rain, he found himself bedridden the next day with a fever.

Stewart had barked orders to the servants as if he were still in the army, demanding watered-down broth, blankets and warming bricks. The servants tiptoed quietly around Jonathan's room and spoke in hushed tones, for Stewart had promised an immediate sacking to anyone who disturbed Jonathan's slumber.

Jonathan, sitting in bed, blew his nose for probably the hundredth time that day and sighed. "Stewart!" he called. "Stewart!"

A few moments later Stewart's heavy footfalls sounded outside of the door. "Jonathan!" he said, breathless. "What is wrong? Do I need to call the doctor again?"

No! "I'm fine," Jonathan said, crossing his arms. "Roberts just left and said you promised to sack him if I got out of bed."

Stewart smiled and leaned one shoulder up against the doorway. "If I just told you to stay in bed, you'd probably be outside... gardening or something."

Jonathan frowned. "I don't care for gardening. But you cannot keep me here in bed."

"Apparently, I can," Stewart said, moving into the bedroom. "But I will compromise. If you are feeling well enough this afternoon we will take a short walk in the garden, or we can go sit in the library."

"Both of those," Jonathan countered, sniffing. He covertly touched the handkerchief to his nose.

Stewart sat down on the bed and felt Jonathan's head as if he were a boy. "No fever," he said. "We can start with the walk in garden first. It will probably do you good to get some fresh air."

"I feel like I'm being mothered," Jonathan murmured. "I'm a 35 year-old man, you know."

"Yes, one who had an attack of his heart two weeks ago, and then decided to go walking in a rainstorm shortly thereafter."

"It wasn't raining when I left," Jonathan reminded him.

"Nevertheless, you are staying in bed until you are well, if not for your sake, then for mine. God knows if you collapse again my own poor heart is going to go out."

Guilt washed through Jonathan. "I'm sorry," he said.

"No, no more sorries," Stewart said, holding up his hand, his eyebrows narrowed.

"Er... I'm sorry that I'm sorry?" Jonathan said, looking at Stewart out of the corner of his eye.

Stewart sat, staring at Jonathan, the edges of his mouth twitching, until he finally broke out into laughter. He put his head in his hand and gently rubbed his forehead. "Whatever am I going to do with you?" he asked, shaking his head slowly.

It seemed to be a trending question. "You make me sound as if I am some poor stray off the street," Jonathan said.

"I might make the argument that you were."

"And that would make you my benevolent master, then?" Jonathan smirked. He knew that somehow the idea was wrong, but truly, that didn't sound terrible at all.

"Something like that," Stewart said, sitting up straight and petting Jonathan's head like a dog.

Jonathan pursed his lips. All right, so he didn't care to be treated like a pet, then. Good to know. Lightly batting Stewart's arm away, Jonathan said, "You've been shaving yourself again, haven't you?"

"Yes," Stewart said. "I did it for ten years while in the army. Just because you've been doing it for the past five doesn't mean I don't remember how."

"Well, you missed a spot," Jonathan frowned. "If you go to your club, be sure to do a cursory review of your chin before you step out."

"You're just upset because I did not need your help this morning," Stewart teased.

"No." *Yes.*

"All right then," Stewart said, rising from the bed, wincing only slightly as he put his full weight onto his knee. "I will come back for you after luncheon, then, and we will take a short stroll. What should I have Cook send you up?"

"Food," Jonathan all but growled. "If I have one more bowl of broth I believe I shall float away."

Stewart chuckled and stepped out the door. "Food," he repeated. "I'll let Cook know your culinary requirements." He shut the door behind him.

Jonathan watched the door close, then stared out the window for a short time before throwing his head back and groaning.

He was so bored!

CHAPTER NINETEEN

Was he dead? No, he didn't feel dead. Perhaps he was dreaming.

Jonathan rarely dreamed; sleep was usually merely a dark void, sometimes merely six to eight hours of calm darkness, sometimes an oblivion into which he could escape the pain of his melancholia. He often found himself jealous of other men who claimed to have erotic dreams about mistresses, actresses, or even young virginal misses who came to them during their sleep, although he did feel thankful to be spared the nightmares of reliving battles that he knew some of his fellow officers still faced. So when Jonathan dreamed of Stewart, he did not move, as he did not know what to do or to expect.

It was dark in his dream, which he found to be somewhat annoyed over. Certainly if he was going to dream about Stewart it should be light, in the middle of the day. Dream Stewart was also not holding him, but sitting on the side of his bed, quite chaste, and dressed in his shirt and breeches. Being dressed was yet another aspect of the dream that Jonathan would have changed, had he known how to do so. But as Jonathan felt Dream Stewart gently caress his face and hair, he found he didn't really care too much about the dark or about what clothing Dream Stewart was wearing.

To be true, all Dream Stewart was doing was lightly brushing back his hair out of his face, as one might a child. Still, it felt so wonderful, after pondering for years what it might feel like, Jonathan knew- he just *knew* it would feel like this. But should it not feel like how he had thought, how he had imagined it to be? It was his dream, was it not? Jonathan reached up and gently took Dream Stewart's hand, setting a soft kiss to the inside of his palm, then braced himself on one elbow and reached up to softly stroke Dream Stewart's face with the back of his knuckle. He could barely see Dream Stewart's face in the darkening twilight- drat his dreams for not setting the scene somewhere more romantic than his dark bedroom. But while he could barely make out his visage, he could hear Stewart's sharp intake of breath, smell his spicy cologne and feel the rough stubble of his evening whiskers on his hand. He had all of his other senses- he would make do with this Dream Stewart for now.

Gently moving his hand back to Dream Stewart's head, he drew his lover to his lips, gently setting them against his. Dream Stewart was stiff, as he knew he would be, but his lips were soft, and Jonathan lovingly kissed him before gingerly tracing his tongue across Dream Stewart's lips and finally, finally, into his mouth, hesitantly tasting him.

Dream Stewart did not kiss him back right away, but after a harsh intake of breath, threw himself into the kiss, and Jonathan found himself bracing himself harder onto his elbow, lest Dream Stewart throw him to the bed. But this was his dream, and he had some things he wanted to try before the morning and Dream Stewart was gone. He gentled the kiss some, and moved his hand down, across Dream Stewart's back- the muscles did feel as taunt and hard as he had imagined- and tugged out the crisp white shirt, feeling the soft skin beneath.

Jonathan gently caressed Dream Stewart's body with his right hand, slowly moving his hand up and down Dream Stewart's back, causing Dream Stewart's breath to hitch. Jonathan deepened the kiss on one of those breaths, and Dream Stewart moaned loudly. Dear God in heaven, Jonathan thought, it is better than I had hoped. He felt his entire body ache for this man, and prayed that no one would pound on his door and ask him to wake up.

No one pounded, no sun rose to wake him, no errant dog or newspaper boy below called to disturb him from his slumber. Perhaps this is heaven, Jonathan thought, and sat up quickly, moving his kisses to Dream Stewart's neck and throat. Jonathan licked the spiny whiskers with his tongue, enthralled with the taste of the dream man in his arms. "Stewart," he murmured, moving back to Dream Stewart's mouth.

"I... Jonathan... what?" Dream Stewart mumbled.

But it wasn't Dream Stewart who answered, Jonathan realized. It was Stewart Stewart.

Jonathan quickly pushed himself up onto a sitting position and back onto the bed. Oh, no. Oh, no, no, no. "Stewart, I- I'm so... I didn't..." Jonathan trailed off as Stewart sat, bracing himself with one hand on the bed.

"I was dreaming," was obviously the truth, but how to explain that he was dreaming of being with another man seemed the trickier part. "It was dark and I thought you were a woman," did not seem fair to either him or Stewart.

98

"Stewart, I..." Jonathan began again, but no words, no explanation came out. Namely, because he had none. "I apologize- I thought, you were, I... thought I was dreaming," he babbled, getting to his feet and pushing past Stewart, who did not look up, did not look over at Jonathan. *Oh, how he must despise me,* Jonathan thought.

Jonathan paused for a moment, wanting to comfort his friend, wanting to promise him it would not happen again. "So... sorry... Stewart," he said, stumbling across the floor to the doorway. "I did not... I... sorry," he muttered, and ran out of the room.

Stewart, however, merely blinked, pushing himself into a full sitting position. *What the hell just happened?* was first and foremost on his brain. He had come to check on Jonathan, as he had, after all, talked him into not just a walk in the garden but also time in the library. Stewart had sat on the bed, watching Jonathan sleep as he imagined parents did their children. He felt no paternal feelings for Jonathan, even though somehow he had an innate urge almost from meeting the young man to care for him and protect him. He had gently brushed the blond hair out of Jonathan's face with a smile; he should suggest that Jonathan cut his hair tomorrow. Of course, that was probably why Jonathan had not had his own cut, to try to put the idea of a haircut into his head. Stewart had smiled; Jonathan's subtle mind games worked only when one did not realize he was being played. But still, he supposed he did need a haircut.

He saw when Jonathan blinked his eyes open, but he did not stop gently stroking Jonathan's forehead. He wasn't sure why. He should have just stood up right then and there and cleared his throat and ask if Jonathan needed anything and walked out. But instead, he continued to stroke Jonathan's forehead and cheek, the silence of the evening magnifying all of the other subtle sounds in the room.

When Jonathan had sat up and touched him, Stewart almost drew back. But he didn't, although in that also he wasn't sure why. And when Jonathan kissed him, he definitely should have drawn back, should have stood up, should have stopped whatever it was that they were doing. But he didn't.

And now... now where the hell was Jonathan? Stewart sighed, standing up from the bed, limping lightly to the hallway. Silence permeated the house; it was too early yet for servants to be up and about, and he did not feel like going room-to-room to challenge

Jonathan on what just happened. Especially, thought Stewart, as he was not sure *what* the hell had just happened.

No, he would go to bed, and he and Jonathan would talk later that day, when it was light, when there were no more shadows to hide them.

CHAPTER TWENTY

"Pressed to death," was more fitting of someone accused of witchcraft, but at that moment, Jonathan was fairly certain that would be his fate. The mail coach lurched and lumbered unevenly, and Jonathan felt himself squished on one side by a very portly gentleman on his left, and then a well-endowed woman on his right. He sighed, righting himself. Perhaps if he was... *of that persuasion*, he would find at least part of the ride enjoyable, but as it was he could not appreciate the sunburned cleavage pushed up against him. *Subtlety, my dear, try for subtlety,* he wanted to admonish her, but remained silent, trying instead to keep his eyes down or ahead of him. He kept his eyes mostly down, however, staring at his hands, as the forward-facing seat was taken up by a woman with two children, a young boy and a small waif of a girl. The boy kept making faces at him whenever he caught his eye, and while in other cases he might have been amused by the boy's antics, he found no desire to be thusly diverted.

He had not known where to go when he left the townhouse, but knew that, if nothing else, he would not see Stewart again. He could not face having his friend look at him in disgust and contempt, now that he knew what he was. Instead, he slipped out of the house, stalking the streets like a footpad, finally taking shelter in a small cafe. Later that afternoon found him slipping back into the house when he knew Stewart would be away. He had quickly packed a small trunk and his valise, wondering if he should leave a note so Stewart would not expect him back. Impulsively, he scribbled a few lines and left them on Stewart's desk in the library before leaving, taking great care to avoid Roberts and Mrs. Banks.

He had hailed a hackney, and decided the mail coach was the cheapest and most efficient way to go. When the man at the counter had asked him where to, however, Jonathan had looked at him dumbly. Where would he go?

"Uh... where is that one going?" he asked, motioning to the coach behind him that was being loaded with trunks and mail bags.

"Dover."

"Dover it is, then," said Jonathan. Yes, he could go to Dover and then take a packet boat across to France. Maybe he would travel the continent, now that Napoleon was dead. Go see the sights, the museums, things he had never gotten to see while he and Stewart were on the battlefield....

Stewart.

The coach finally slowed and drew to a stop, shaking Jonathan out of his memories, and the driver barked out a town Jonathan had never heard of. This would probably be the last stop before reaching Dover, and then what? Jonathan assumed he could take the ferry to France and then maybe travel down to Spain. He wondered what the Spanish countryside looked when not being blown apart by cannon fire and littered with dead bodies. It probably smelled more pleasant, anyway.

All of the passengers save the portly man exited the coach to stretch their legs, and Jonathan looked about at the squalor of the little town. It reminded him much of the town in which he grew up, which did not bode well for the town, as he had very few good memories of his childhood.

"Oy! Guv!" the boy on the back of the coach yelled, pointing to Jonathan's valise. This yours?"

"Yes," Jonathan said, walking to the back of the coach.

"Can ye' carry it inside with ye?" the boy asked. "We be takin' on a new passenger, and there's no room for 'is trunk."

Jonathan mentally sighed. Yes, obviously the fates had determined that he had not been nearly uncomfortable enough thus far. "Fine," he said. "Give me the valise."

"Very good, guv," the boy said, handing the valise down to Jonathan. Another boy walked up to the coach with a large trunk. It looked almost as large as he was.

"Oh, here," said Jonathan, "let me help you." With a grunt, he picked up the trunk and placed it on top of his on the coach, where the boy lashed it down. "Many thanks, guv," he smiled, most of his teeth missing.

You should both be in school, not out here working, Jonathan wanted to say. But what was he to do? He could not pay for disadvantaged boys everywhere.

"Here you go," he said to the boys, giving them a penny each, even though he was the one who had done most of the work. "I need to post a letter going back the way of London," Jonathan said. "Where might I do that?"

"Three doors up," said the boy on the ground. "Th' coach t' Lun'un comes by tomorrow."

"Thank you," Jonathan said. "Don't let them leave without me."

"Will do," they said in unison, and Jonathan noticed that they appeared to be brothers under all of their dirt.

Jonathan was just returning when he saw the driver whip up the horses.

"Wait!" he cried, waving one hand as the other hand carried his valise, "Stop!"

As he ran to catch the mail coach, he saw the portly man peer out the window at him. Certainly he would alert the driver! thought Jonathan. But no, the fat man merely smiled smugly and sat back, and the coach flew off in a hail of dirt and pebbles towards Dover.

"Bastard," Jonathan muttered under his breath. He watched the coach disappear in a flurry of dust, and trudged back towards the town. The man probably was pleased with being able to sit right next to the woman with the overflowing chest, he figured.

"I tried to stop 'im, I did!" cried the boy as Jonathan stomped past, but Jonathan was so annoyed he did not stop, but merely kept walking.

After inquiring when the next mail coach would be- in a week- he walked to the alehouse and found an empty seat at the cleanest table he could find, ordering a beer when he was told they had nothing stronger. He mentally saluted Dr. Lambrose with his drink before downing almost half of it, sitting back in the uncomfortable wooden chair. An entire week in this insufferable, dirty little town would certainly be the equivalent of any hell he could have otherwise devised for himself. *Perhaps it's what you deserve,* he heard his conscience tell him.

Jonathan pushed the thought away. It was thoughts like those that led to his melancholia. While he had easily found a way to divert them while living with Stewart, he knew that they would now be more difficult to ignore. Shoving them away as quickly as they came was the only way he would get through the next week. And then....

And then, what? What else do you plan to do with your pathetic life?

Jonathan took another swig of the watered-down ale and sighed. This was going to be more difficult than he thought.

It was several hours later that Jonathan stumbled from the alehouse towards the inn that the proprietor had recommended with a knowing grin on his face that Jonathan did not understand. He had gotten himself quite drunk and was quite satisfied with the numb feeling that accompanied his present state. He tripped across the road to where the alehouse owner had pointed him, coming across what looked to be a run-down inn. It was ghastly, Jonathan could tell, even through his drunken stupor.

"Hello!" he called at the darkened entrance. "I am looking for a room." He swayed a bit, placing his hand on the doorway, which chipped and splintered slightly. "Ow!" he murmured, and peered down at his hand. Good Lord! Both of his hands had splinters! No, no, just the two left hands. Jonathan used both of his right hands to try to pull the wooden slivers out of his skin, narrowing his eyes to try to focus.

"May I help ye?" a young woman bobbed a curtsy as she came down the narrow staircase in front of him.

"I've a splinter," Jonathan wailed pathetically, holding up a hand. Wait, no, two hands.

"Ah, ye' probably put yer hand on the side there, didn't ye?" the young miss said, walking towards him. "That doorway's seen better days, it has. Let me see if I can help ye'." She gently took Jonathan's soft hand and placed it in her own more callused palm. For some reason, Jonathan was reminded of his mother, and smiled, closing his eyes.

"Yer lucky yer skin is so soft," the young woman said, gently pulling out the splinters. "They be coming out without any problem. Just one more... there. Right as rain," she smiled, patting his palm.

Jonathan curled his fingers into his palm. "Thank you," he whispered, opening his eyes again and taking a step back. "How much do I owe you?"

"For takin' out a bit of wood from yer hand? I believe that service comes with the room," she said, her eyes bright. At least, Jonathan was fairly certain they were bright. His eyes could not quite focus.

"The mail coach has abandoned me, so I'll need a room for the week," Jonathan said with a frown. He picked up the valise he had dropped and waited for the woman to respond.

"Oh, yer the gentleman they left behind! Oh, they were quite in the wrong to do that!" she exclaimed. "Luke said that he tried to tell the coachman you were coming back."

"Ah, the young man with the trunk," Jonathan said. "Yes, unfortunately the coachman apparently had other plans for the afternoon."

She made him sign the register, and after doing so he looked up at the staircase expectantly. "Well, let me take you up to your room, then," she said, and turned to go back up the dark staircase. Jonathan had to step at an angle in order to place his feet on the steps, and decided right then that there was no way he was going to make it back down while inebriated without breaking his neck. He gripped his valise more tightly in his hand.

"Right through here," the woman said, opening the door to what might have been at one time a perfectly serviceable room. It had seen many years of use, however, and Jonathan was reminded of when he was in the army, sleeping in barns and on the cold ground before he had met Stewart. Ah, Stewart.... He sighed, and felt his drunkenness start to fade, giving way to painful awareness. "It will do. Thank you, Miss...."

"Wells," she said. "Mrs. Juliana Wells."

"Of course. Thank you Mrs. Wells," Jonathan said, stepping into the room and putting his valise on the bed. The floor looked a bit circumspect.

"Would you like a bath sent up?" she asked.

Probably a half-barrel with lye, thought Jonathan harshly. "Uh, no, thank you Mrs. Wells," he said. "I would not want to trouble you. Perhaps merely some hot water?"

"Certainly," she said, pulling to door closed. "I'll send Luke right up."

Jonathan sat on the edge of the mattress and sighed. At least it appeared that there were no bugs living in the bed, and the mattress was not filled with straw. He supposed he should be thankful for small favors.

Stewart would be livid in this situation, he knew, and Jonathan would be trying his best to make light of things in order to keep his friend from lashing out at anyone and everyone in his way. Jonathan leaned over and put his head in his hands. Would nothing stop reminding him of what he had lost?

A light knock tapped on the door. "Come in!" he said, thinking that Stewart would have barked an "Enter!" instead.

"Beggin' yer pardon, m'lord," said the boy who he had helped earlier that day. He supposed this was the illustrious Luke.

"Yes, Luke, please, put the water right there next to what I believe is supposed to be a dresser."

"Yes, m'lord," Luke said, lugging the bucket of water across the room.

"And I am not a lord," said Jonathan. "You may call me sir or Lieutenant."

"Yer a Lieutenant?" the boy's eyebrows shot up in surprise. "But why aren't ye' wearin' yer red coat?"

"Well, I am not currently engaged in battle, one, and two, I am retired."

"Then why are ye' dressed like a lord?"

"It is amazing, but true, that given enough money, a tailor will make you whatever clothes you desire," Jonathan said, a hint of a smile on his lips.

"Me fadder's in th' infintry. Do ye' know 'im?" Luke asked.

Probably wouldn't be able to tell him if he did. "I confess I do not know. What regiment is he in?"

"'E's in the 32nd Foot," Luke said proudly.

"Ah, under Major Hicks, then," Jonathan supplied.

"No, it was Commander Wellington," Luke corrected, standing a bit taller. Jonathan smiled, not wanting to correct the boy. He was correct after a fashion, after all.

"Was your father at Waterloo, then?"

"Aye, 'e was," said Luke. "An' when 'e comes home, 'e'll be sure to tell me all of 'is stories of battle."

Or he'll spend the rest of his life reliving the atrocities he witnessed on that battlefield, thought Jonathan.

"I'm sure he is quite proud of you, m'boy, helping out your mother. Now, get along, and I'm sure I'll see you in the morning."

"'Course, m'lord... er, I mean, Lieutenant," Luke smiled and ran out.

Jonathan stood and closed the door that Luke had left open, took off his jacket and threw it haphazardly onto a rickety chair that looked as if it were going to collapse under the weight of it, then sat back down on the bed, ignoring the hot water. With a sigh, he slipped under the covers still dressed in his shirt and breeches, and waited for sleep to rescue him from his interminable pain.

CHAPTER TWENTY-ONE

"It was the getting up that killed him." Or, at least that was what Jonathan was fairly sure would happen. He wanted to stay in his nice cocoon of sheltered blankets, where it was safe, and he could drift back into sleep and forget about Stewart, about kissing Stewart....

Jonathan rolled over to his back and placed his hand over his head, staring at the cracked and stained ceiling above. If only he had managed to keep his urges to himself, then he would be waking up in his own bed right now, or even chastising Stewart in his choice of waistcoats. Stupid, stupid, stupid! He *never* dreamed. Ever. Why would he think that night would be any different?

Because you wanted it to be.

Yes, that was the truth. And dammit, for a few seconds of indulging his urges, he was in some god-awful inn in some horrible little town, going God knew where. Tears leaked out of his eyes, and he allowed himself to engage in self-pity for a short time before taking a deep breath. If he did not get up, the melancholia would begin to take over, and he no longer had Stewart to help him with that; if anything, not having Stewart in his life would make it even worse.

Forcing himself to get out of bed, Jonathan dressed as quickly as possible in order to reduce the temptation to fall back onto the mattress. The fact that he was hungry helped; it gave him a purpose, as insignificant as it might be at that moment. Moving as carefully as he could down the stairs, he saw a figure in black bent over at the front of the entryway. "Oh, Mrs. Wells," he said, "Where might the dining area be?"

The figure stood up, but Jonathan was quickly aware that it was not Mrs. Wells; it looked like some deformed creature out of one of Mrs. Banks' novels. One of her eyes was white and the other wandered about the socket. *Oh dear God it's the Graeae*, thought Jonathan, forcing himself not to step back or even run from the room screaming.

"Mrs. Wells, she 's only 'ere las' night ta help," said the ancient woman. "She comes when ah'm not feelin' up t' workin'."

Jonathan was surprised the woman in front of him was feeling well enough to be alive, much less working. "Oh, well, I see," he said. "I, uh... wondered... breakfast... food... Icangotothealehouse," he said quickly.

"Oh, no," said the woman. "Ye' jus' sit down in t' parlor right behind ye'. Ah have some food on t' side table fer ye an' me udder guests." As she finished her sentence, she began a hacking cough that made Jonathan's heart grip for a reason other its usual cause.

He was fairly certain he would rather starve.

"I thank you," he said, "I will go in there now. But I was thinking of walking around the town this morning, so I will most likely just find something to put into my pockets. Thank you, Missus..." he paused, hoping for Mrs. Wells' sake that this was not her relation.

"Beadsley," she croaked. "Mrs. Beadsley. Mr. Beadsley, he passed 'bout ten years ago, but I never kent to marry 'gain."

"Ah... I am sorry for your loss, Mrs. Beadsley. I should go have breakfast now. Pray, excuse me." Jonathan gave a quick bow before heading into the parlor, grabbing an apple- the only thing he assumed was safe- and slipping out of a side door.

"If'n ye wan' t' come back fer dinner, I do make an excellen' tart!" she called before breaking out into a coughing fit again.

Jonathan fairly flew out of the inn, scrambling out into the street before he calmed himself and forced himself into a stroll. There was not much to the town, as he had found the night before, but at least he was outside, the air was fresh, and it was not raining. Oh, thank heaven it was not raining. Perhaps he could find a place to live where it never rained. Italy, perhaps, or maybe he could travel down to Egypt. See the pyramids, ride a camel. Jonathan smiled. Stewart would love the pyramids and hate the camel.

Damn it, stop, he commanded himself.

Jonathan wandered down a quiet little lane, munching his apple, trying to focus on what sightseeing he might do. He could do the Grand Tour, about 15 years late, and visit Venice, Rome, and travel down to Greece. Oh, no- the Turks were still in Greece. Maybe just skip over that country, then. Keeping his thoughts focused on what sights he might see, he almost did not see the blur streak in front of him before it was too late.

"What, well, ho there!" he said, grabbing the blur, spinning it around.

"Git off!" the blur yelled, squirming.

"Luke?" he said, gently setting the boy down.

"Luke's me brudder," the boy said. "I'm Mark."

"Of course you are," Jonathan said. He assumed there was a David and Matthew gallivanting about somewhere. "Where are you going in such haste?"

"Nun a' yer business!" Mark said.

Jonathan stared at Mark for a moment, then shrugged. "I suppose it isn't. Good day, then." He had begun to walk on when Mark yelled out, "Kin ye' read?"

"What?" Jonathan asked, turning around.

"Kin ye' read?" Mark said in an exasperated tone.

Jonathan knew better than to say, of course, and instead replied, "I am able to read. Do you need something read for you?"

"It's fer me ma," Mark said hesitantly.

"Well, then, let's to her," Jonathan said, "I find myself in need of diversion, anyway. Lead the way, young sir."

"I'm notta' sir."

"Ah, you are once again correct. I should say, young master. Now, where is your mother?"

"She's in th' cottage," Mark said. "Ye' talk funny, like th' udder gents from London."

"So I do," Jonathan agreed. "Perhaps you could show me the way?" Mark nodded, and trotted in front of him, looking back every so often to see if Jonathan was still following. Jonathan refused to run, but walked quickly, his long stride easily keeping up as the boy scampered up the dirt road.

They turned into a gravel lane where a very humble cottage stood, a perfect picture of the English country, complete with a small brown pony munching grass to the side.

"Me mudder's in 'ere," Mark said, throwing the door open and rushing inside.

Jonathan did not rush after Mark, but calmly walked to the doorway and peered in. "Er... Mrs. Wells?" he asked. "Uh... Mark said you may need some assistance."

Mrs. Wells hurried to the door, her hair falling out of her cap, her eyes red. "Oh, dear," she said. "I'm so sorry. Mark should have never bothered ye."

"It's no bother, Mrs. Wells," Jonathan said. "Mark said you perhaps needed some help?"

"Well, yes, then, if ye're a mind," she said. "I've received a letter today."

Please don't have it be a missive stating that your husband is dead.

Instead, Mrs. Wells pulled a short note from her apron pocket and gave it to Jonathan. Jonathan cringed as he first read the note, then visibly relaxed; it was a demand for payment, he noted, for rents on the cottage.

"I know it says I must pay," she wailed. "But I can barely keep enough food on the table. Mr. Wells sends home his pay when he can, but the army hasn't paid him in months. I even started workin' at the inn a few days a week." Jonathan frowned; he knew firsthand that the army was often notoriously late in paying their soldiers.

"Mrs. Wells," Jonathan said, trying to ignore the tears coming down her face, "pray tell, who owns this cottage?"

"It belongs to my husband," she cried, finally blotting away her tears. "T'was his before we were married. This is where he grew up. Why, what does it say?"

The idea of having grown up in this miserable little town explained why he wanted to leave, thought Jonathan, although he supposed the cottage was serviceable enough from what he could see from the doorway.

"Mrs. Wells, I know you do not know me, but may I borrow this piece of paper?" asked Jonathan.

"Well, I dunno," she said hesitantly.

"I can talk Mark along with me, and he can return the paper to you," Jonathan promised.

"Oh, well than I suppose that would be alright," she said. "Do you think you can help us?"

God save him. "Yes, I do believe I can," said Jonathan. "Do you think you can fetch Mark for me?"

"Yes, yes, of course," she said, and turned back into the house. Jonathan walked down the small stone path that led to the street, followed by Mark who scurried out of the door, his mother behind him. She stood at the doorway, and Jonathan smiled and gave a cursory wave before heading back to town, the little boy at his heels.

"Where we goin'?" Mark asked.

"I need you to tell me where I might find a... Mr. Hetherington," said Jonathan, staring at the missive.

"Oh, yes, 'e has a shop in town," said Mark. "Tha's where ma usually has her letters read."

Convenient, thought Jonathan, his step quickening. "One more question," Jonathan said. "Who's the local magistrate?

When they got to the town, Jonathan sent Mark to fetch the magistrate and continued on to where the boy said he could find Mr. Hetherington. Finding his small shop at the edge of the town, Jonathan rang the small bell that was sitting on the counter.

"Ah, Mrs. Wells!" a man said from the back. "I was expecting you!"

"Not Mrs. Wells," said Jonathan flatly.

"Oh, I do apologize," a small man appeared, smoothing a few hairs across his balding head. He was dressed in an atrocious brown suit that fit snugly over his large frame. "How may I help you, sir?"

"I was wondering if you could help me with this?" Jonathan said, placing the missive on the counter.

"I, er... well, this is a demand for payment on rent on the cottage," said Mr. Hetherington nervously.

"Really?" said Jonathan sarcastically. "And do you believe me to be an idiot? Mr. Wells owns that cottage outright."

"Oh, but he doesn't," said Mr. Hetherington hesitantly. "You see, just before he returned to service, he took out a small loan. It hasn't been paid back, you see. I have the paperwork right here." Hetherington walked to the back of the small store and pulled open a file cabinet. "Oh, yes, see here... he took out a loan for five pounds last month when he was here on leave."

"Your demand for payment lists says she owes thirty pounds or she'll forfeit ownership of the cottage!"

"Well, you see sir, there is the interest on the loan," Hetherington said, wringing his hands together.

Jonathan narrowed his eyes. "Twenty-five pounds interest on a five pound note? What interest is that?"

"Oh, well, you see, it's all listed right there on the paperwork, that if the original loan is not paid off in two weeks, the percentage will go up incrementally."

"You showed this to Mr. Wells?"

"Oh, yes, and Mrs. Wells," Hetherington said, nodding.

"Am I to assume neither of them are literate?" Jonathan roared.

"Well," said Mr. Hetherington, taking a step back.

"I am going to tell you what I am going to do," said Jonathan in a low, dark voice, which seemed to strike greater fear in Hetherington than his shouting had. "I am going to pay the thirty pounds," Mr. Hetherington looked a bit relieved, "but I have summoned the magistrate." Mr. Hetherington began to look pale again. "And you are going to explain to him how you tried to take advantage of a soldier who fought at Waterloo." Jonathan got a small thrill in watching Hetherington break out in a sweat.

It was several hours later when Jonathan walked wearily back to the inn and climbed the ridiculously steep and narrow stairs up to his room. All of his energy had been depleted; after he had explained how Hetherington had been scamming Mrs. Wells, they had gotten him to confess to doing the same to others as well. Mrs. Wells had been terribly angry when Jonathan had told her what had happened, but thanked him and invited him to dinner, which he had politely refused. Although his wallet was now thirty pounds lighter (a considerable sum, that), he had no interest in taking food out of her boys' mouths.

Jonathan knew he should feel proud of himself for exposing such a man, but all he felt was tired. He stripped and crawled into the uncomfortable bed. He wanted to tell Stewart what he had done, hear Stewart's outrage at Mr. Hetherington's gall. He wanted to hear Stewart's reaction when he told him that the magistrate had jailed Mr. Hetherington, and ask him if he knew any judges to ensure his sentence was the longest possible. But most of all, he just wanted to sit in his chair by the fireplace next to Stewart, pretending to gag as Stewart smoked his pipe, and read aloud whatever book Stewart had chosen that night. He wanted his life back. He wanted Stewart back.

You can't have Stewart back. Your entire friendship was based upon a lie.

Was it? If he had never initially been attracted to Stewart, would he have wanted to be his friend? Yes, he told himself. He had liked Stewart, not just his handsome face.

If Stewart knew what you were, he would never have helped you. He would never have been your friend.

Jonathan found he could not argue with that.

You were never Stewart's friend.

Jonathan squeezed his eyes closed, praying for sleep, but the thoughts continued to barrage him. He was too tired to fight them, and instead lay in the cold, dark bed, consumed with cold, dark thoughts.

CHAPTER TWENTY-TWO

I am going to kill him, Stewart thought. On Jonathan's tombstone they would write, "Murdered by Retired Colonel Stewart Ainsley, Earl of Durnley." Stewart frowned; it would look odd to have his name on Jonathan's tombstone. Perhaps he would just write, "Murdered by his long-suffering friend." Yes, that sounded more dramatic, anyway.

Stewart sighed heavily as he stared out at the dismal landscape as his carriage bumped over unkempt roads. When Jonathan had not come back the morning after... *that night*, he was concerned. When he was still missing that afternoon, he was worried. When Jonathan had not returned or sent word by that evening, Stewart had torn apart the house looking for any sort of clue to Jonathan's whereabouts, finally finding a short note in his library from Jonathan telling him not to worry. Bah! he had thought, and had turned it over and over, looking for some clue, something that would indicate where Jonathan had gone. There was nothing, just the words, "Don't worry about me. -Jonathan."

In Jonathan's study, however, Stewart had found a letter on very cheap paper from a woman thanking Jonathan for sending her money. He gave the direction to Henry and early the next morning they were on the way to some town he had never heard of before.

Certainly Jonathan did not keep a mistress out here in the middle of nowhere, days from London, now would he? When would he even find the time to visit her? Truly, save for this month, he could not count but a handful of days when they had been separated.

The carriage finally slowed, and Stewart looked out at the small town as the carriage drew closer to it. A few boys and a dog began running after them, and Stewart sat back against the seat. The town apparently did not have many outsiders come through.

When they reached the main section of the town, Stewart pounded the ceiling with his cane and called to Henry. "Find what looks to be like a hotel or public stables," he called.

A few moments passed when Henry called back through the window, "I think this is it, my lord. Are you sure you want to stop here?"

No. No, I'm not sure. I'm not sure why I'm gallivanting all over England for a man who obviously does not wish to be found.

"Yes, Henry," Stewart said in his best "I'm an Earl, and so I know what I'm doing" voice. The footman lowered the stairs for him, and Stewart used his cane to brace himself as he stepped out. "I'm going to see if I can find someone who might know where Lieutenant Redding might be. Why don't you put the horses up in the stables, get something to eat? I'm not sure how long we'll be here," Stewart finished, handing Henry a few coins.

"Ay, m'lord," Henry said, and the footman quickly closed the door and hopped on the back as Henry drove the carriage around to the stables.

Stewart looked around, assessing the town. It was small, with a few shops, two pubs, and not much else. He decided to try one of the pubs for information, and as he turned, he bumped into a small blur of golden curls.

"Ooof!" Stewart said, catching himself with his cane as his knee went out. "Pray pardon, young miss."

"Oh, it was my fault," she said. "I was running to meet you. I saw the carriage come up, and I just knew it would be you!"

This little thing could not be more than 16 or 17. Jonathan had a 17 year-old mistress? No, that didn't make sense. Perhaps his child? She did resemble Jonathan quite a bit, and it would explain the money. Stewart felt a pain of betrayal, remembering when Jonathan had said he would never have children.

"I am looking for someone," Stewart said. "You may know him? Lieutenant Jonathan Redding?"

"Of course. I know you. You're Stewart," said the young girl, batting her eyelashes precociously.

Stewart furrowed his brows. "Why, yes, I am, young miss. Lord Stewart Ainsley, Earl of Durnley, at your service." He sketched a short bow. "And at the risk of my impertinence, as you know me, may I have the honor of your name?"

"Jonathan says ladies are not supposed to talk to men unless someone else has introduced them."

"Why, yes, that is true," Stewart said slowly, his eyes narrowing, "but I believe Jonathan has introduced me to you via his letters, is that correct?"

"I guess,.," the young girl said, clearly thinking of the broach of etiquette, which Stewart was thinking was far too convenient a reason for her coyness.

"So, as I have been introduced to you, now I may take your hand, and you may tell me your name," Stewart said with his most charming smile.

The girl giggled, and gave Stewart her hand with a mischievous grin. Stewart forced himself not to roll his eyes, knowing that this was what she had been after. She had to be a relation of Jonathan's, to get him to easily do things he did not want to do, and think it was his idea in the process. "I'm Susanna Redding," she said, giggling again, and almost shrieked when he lightly kissed her knuckles before releasing her. "Jonathan is my big brother."

Right about the sister, then. Somehow the fact that she wasn't Jonathan's child pleased Stewart to no end. Was this little town where Jonathan had grown up? "A pleasure, my dear. Your dress is lovely, by the by. Has Jonathan come by recently?" Stewart asked as innocently as possible. "I wanted to give him something, but I do not have his forwarding address."

Susanna giggled again. "Oh, no, he is in a town outside of Dover. Why do you ask? Didn't you send him there?"

"Pardon?" Stewart asked.

"Didn't you send him there on official military business?" Susanna said very slowly, as if Stewart were dense.

Official military business? What had Jonathan been telling her?

"He said he could not say why he was sent there. Just that it was official military business," Susanna repeated.

"Ah," Stewart said. Official military business meant, *None of your business why I left London, Missy.* Playing along, Stewart said, "Yes, you know, he really should not have even told you that. I do hope that you've kept that information to yourself."

"Oh, yes," Susanna said, not realizing how she had been manipulated. Ha! Take that, Redding family! thought Stewart, who took Susanna's arm with a practiced move and placed it on his own and began walking up the street. "No one talks about Jonathan, anyway," Susanna added, "So you don't have to worry about me blabbing to anyone else."

"No? Why is that?" Stewart asked nonchalantly.

"Because Papa got angry with him and made him leave. He even tried to get Jonathan's birth record erased, but of course the magistrate said that was illegal."

Stewart had always commiserated with Jonathan when discussing difficult father figures, but this was impossible. Getting his birth record erased?

"First we weren't allowed to talk about Mama 'cuz Papa had her committed to the 'sylum, then we weren't allowed to talk about Jonathan." Susanna sighed deeply. "But nobody ever really brings them up, so I guess it's not that hard." Jonathan's mother had been committed? The girl was a veritable fountain of knowledge regarding Jonathan, thought Stewart.

"I'm sorry to hear about your mother," Stewart offered.

"Papa sent her away after I was born," Susanna murmured sadly. "She died there, you know."

"Why did your father send her there?" Stewart asked. He knew it was dreadfully rude to inquire, but he assumed Susanna was not as well versed in social etiquette as she should be.

"She suffered from melancholia. Same as Jonathan," Susanna said.

Jonathan suffered from melancholia? "I did not realize... that he did so," Stewart finished lamely.

"Oh, no, not so much anymore," Susanna said. "He said that it's being with you that keeps the melancholia away."

Stewart felt like someone just punched him in the gut.

"I think that's why Papa sent Mama away. Because he felt bad that he couldn't stop the melancholia."

An insightful young thing, Stewart thought. She would be dangerous when she was officially on the marriage mart. If Jonathan would actually let any men near her, that was.

"Papa was awful mad when he found out Jonathan suffered from the melancholia. Not as mad, though, as when the actor told him about what he and Jonathan were doing."

"Actor?"

"He said he wanted Papa to pay him so he wouldn't tell about what he and Jonathan did. My sister said she saw them once together, though. She said all they did was kiss. I don't think it's fair," she said, kicking the dirt with her sturdy shoes. "No one told on my sister when she was caught kissing behind the shed with ol' Billy Mundy."

"No, not fair at all," Stewart murmured. Random thoughts fell into place; small innuendos, a small sigh, a wistful turn of the head Jonathan was gay; that must have been the "falling out" he had with his father. Stewart frowned, assimilating the information, reviewing what Susanna had just said. *Jonathan had been betrayed by his own lover?*

"He's in love with you, you know," Susanna said matter-of-factly.

Stewart choked. "P-pardon?" he asked, looking around to see if anyone had heard, but apparently there were few enough people working in town, and even fewer strolling through it.

"He never said so, you know," Susanna continued, "but I can tell. I think he's been in love with you since he met you in Australia."

"Er, Austria," corrected Stewart.

Susanna shrugged.

In love with him since then? Why, that was 15 years ago!

Giving a little cough, Stewart deftly changed the subject.

"Ah, well, um... Jonathan writes you quite regularly?"

"Oh, Papa doesn't know," Susanna said quickly. "When my other two sisters- they're older, you know- when they were my age, I guess, Jonathan made sure we all had dowries, and sent us all money every month- to buy fripperies, he said. But I mostly use mine to pay the butcher."

He provided dowries for his sisters? Pay the butcher?

"Is that not your father's job?" *For both?*

Susanna shrugged. "Our benefactor often forgets to pay Papa, and Papa often forgets to ask him for money."

"And your brother sends you money regularly?"

Susanna looked up and thought for a moment. "Well, I don't think he sends money to my sisters anymore," she said finally. "They're married," she added.

"I see. One to Billy Mundy?"

"Oh, no," Susanna said, making a face. "He's awful. I don't know what Mary was doing with him, anyway."

Stewart pushed down a smile. "I see. Well, a belated congratulations to them."

"I would have been introduced to you sooner, you know, more formal-like, if Jonathan had been invited to the weddings."

"And why was he not?" His questions were now beyond rude, but the girl did not seem to mind. In fact, she seemed more than eager to ply him with information.

"Oh, on the account that he's a, well... *you know*," said, rolling her eyes.

That Jonathan liked men.

That Jonathan was attracted to men.

And Jonathan was apparently in love with *him*.

"I can see about not being invited to the weddings, but I don't see why they can't even write him. I mean, it's not like anyone would know," Susanna grumbled.

Stewart almost stopped dead on his feet. Luckily, they were in front of a sweet shop, and Susanna turned and looked at the offerings in the window as if it had been planned. Stewart felt his heart break for his friend. Jonathan had been betrayed by his lover. He was in love with him, and he had no idea. His friend had been supporting his family for years, including offering his sister's dowries, and in return they had all but refused contact with him. All except this very coquettish young girl on his arm, that is.

Susanna began walking, apparently not seeing anything of interest, and Stewart fell into step again. "Jonathan doesn't really complain, you know. Well, sometimes, but he won't say anything to my sisters directly. They say he's non-confrontible. Non-confrontional. Non...."

"Non-confrontational," Stewart supplied. Yes, that summed up Jonathan nicely.

"Yes!" Susanna said, relieved. "*That*. But next year Jonathan said I could have a Season, and that your sister is going to sponsor me."

She was? Was she aware of that?

"We are definitely looking forward to your arrival next year," Stewart said diplomatically. "I don't believe London will be the same again after having experienced the likes of you."

Susanna gave a short laugh. "La, but it will be wonderful!" she said, pulling her arm free and twirling around madly for a minute. "I suppose I won't be able to do that in London," she said with a frown.

"No, I don't suppose so," Stewart said evenly.

"Well, then, I should enjoy doing so now, don't you think?" Susanna said with a gleam in her eye.

Stewart chuckled in spite of himself. "Indeed, Miss Redding, indeed you should. Before I leave you, however, I must ask, do you happen to have the direction to where Jonathan is staying? For the... er... important military business, you know."

"Oh, yes!" Susanna said, pulling out an envelope from her reticule. "I just received a letter today. See- it's written right on here. Jonathan always sends his letters in an envelope so I know they're from him. That way I can hide them from Papa."

"He is very thoughtful that way," Stewart said. "May I?"

Susanna handed him the envelope. "You may keep it, Stewart. Oh, no- I should call you Lord Stewart, right?"

Stewart laughed. "You certainly are a breath of fresh air, Miss Redding. Until next Season, then," he said, and sketched another bow over her hand. Susanna blushed, but refrained from giggling too loudly. Stewart then turned and walked back to the hotel and found Henry in the stables.

"Henry," he barked. "Change of plans. We're going to Dover."

CHAPTER TWENTY-THREE

"Death to them who dun't pay the room charges," was written on a small wooden plaque above the rough desk at what apparently passed for an inn in the rustic town where Jonathan was apparently staying. Stewart could not imagine Jonathan staying anywhere so vile, but when he inquired at the alehouse, the proprietor was fairly adamant that it was the only place his friend could be. And so here he was, standing in the entryway of a very filthy, run-down building that appeared to be a converted tavern.

"May I help ye', m'lord?" an elderly woman asked, hobbling up to Stewart. She was dressed all in black, her clothes partly in tatters. She had apparently gone blind in one eye; the color had been leeched from it, leaving only a white film behind. The other eye was a dark brown and appeared normal except that it did not seem to focus on him, but wandered to the left, so she seemed to be looking out over the top of his head. Stewart refrained from shuddering, but just barely.

"Uh, yes," Stewart said, pulling out a sovereign and setting it down on the rickety desk. He pushed it towards the crone with one finger, but did not release it. "I am looking for a young man, middle-aged, blond hair."

The woman eyed the sovereign with a greedy look. At least, Stewart assumed she was looking at the sovereign; it appeared she was looking at his left sleeve.

"Get lots of th' like in 'ere, guv'," the woman said with a husky voice.

Doubtful. "That's unfortunate," Stewart said, sliding the sovereign back this way. The crone's eye moved back to his elbow.

"Well, m'be if ye're more sp'fic 'bout 'ow yer friend looks I ken help ye?" she said, still eyeing (apparently, but he just could not tell) the sovereign.

Stewart pushed the sovereign back across the scarred wooden surface. "He is almost my height, blond, mid-thirties. He would have come in here about a week or so ago."

The woman laughed, "Oh, I think ah ken who yer talkin' 'bout," she said. Stewart forced himself not to roll his eyes or sigh.

"If you would be so good as to take me to him?"

"'E's not in 'is room," she said. "'Sides, I don't ken tis' right, ye' bein' a stranger 'n' all."

Stewart released the sovereign and placed another on top. "Perhaps you could show me to where he has been staying? I will wait for him there," he said in his most lordly tone.

As soon as his fingers released them, the sovereigns were snatched up by gnarled hands. "'Course," she said. "An' if ye' have a mind to stay fer supper, I kin whip up a batch of m' famous tarts." She cackled as she finished, which turned into a hacking cough.

"I appreciate your kind offer, Mrs., uh..."

"Beadsley," the old woman hacked. "Mr. Beadsley, he passed 'bout ten years ago, but I never kent to marry 'gain."

Stewart had nothing to say to that. "Perhaps if you could just show me the room?"

"'Course, 'course," she said, turning around and walking with painstakingly slow steps up the narrow staircase. Stewart followed, resting on his cane as she slowly shuffled her way. "Poor fella' firs' saved th' Wells' house, then af'er jus' didna' come outta' th' room fer days."

Stewart furrowed his brows. "Saved whose house?"

In her guttural brogue, the woman described in detail what happened with Jonathan and Mr. Hetherington. "Well, here 'tis," she said, finally opening the door to Jonathan's room.

There seemed nothing apparently amiss, Stewart noted as he walked in. The bed, as old and lumpy as it apparently was, had been made, and there were no clothes strewn about, which was unusual for Jonathan. Jonathan's valise was placed at the end of the bed, along with a narrow wooden case. Stewart opened it with his back to the door, to find a single-shot pistol, and quickly closed it again.

While his first inclination had been to wait in Jonathan's room, the minute he walked in, all he wanted to do was find his friend and leave. He picked up Jonathan's valise with his free hand, tucking the box under his arm. "Thank you," he said, dropping another sovereign on the bed before picking up his cane and walking out. The woman did not bother to admonish him for taking Jonathan's things, keeping her eye (probably) on the sovereign. She easily let him push past, and he moved to walk down the hall when he paused. There was something amiss, but he just could not put his finger on the cause.

"Mrs. Beadsley," he called out. "Do you know where this man was heading?"

"T' bridge," she cackled. "'E asked if I ken a bridge, an' I said there's one jus' 'appens to be right outside 'a' th' town."

Stewart felt himself grow ice cold. Jonathan's room was clean, nothing out of place. Jonathan's room was always a pigsty. Why would he leave everything so clean and neat, easily picked up, unless....

"Mrs. Beadsley?" he asked. "I need you to tell me exactly where this bridge is."

CHAPTER TWENTY-FOUR

"A coward dies a thousand deaths, a hero but once," was poetic, but Jonathan found that he was not heroic enough to make that final leap of faith into the churning water below. He had finally dragged himself out of bed that morning after staying in almost a week, feigning illness and having food left outside of his door. He had come to the realization last night that he was unable to live without Stewart; the melancholia had too strong a hold on him. The only thought that helped break through was the thought of suicide.

Not that he had ever previously thought seriously of suicide, even in the deepest throes of melancholia. While he would have begged someone else to put a bullet in his head, he would never be able to do so himself, a fact he found out this morning after purchasing a small pistol and returning to his room. What would his sister say? Where would he be buried? Who would clean up the mess? The thought of Mrs. Beadsley scrubbing pieces of his brain from the ceiling and wall was enough for him to place the gun back into the case.

And so he was here, standing on the bridge, staring down at the fast-moving river. It should be easy; just take a step and that was it. The river was moving too swiftly for him to recover from the fall. He would drown quite quickly. Dammit, why could he not take that step?

Jonathan closed his eyes. Perhaps if he did not see what he was doing, it would be easier, but instead of the calm he had expected, he kept hearing Stewart calling him. Must his brain continue to plague him with thoughts of the one man he would never have? Why could he not gain a measure of peace?

Stewart ran towards the bridge as quickly as his knee would allow, his hat in his hand. "Jonathan!" he called repeatedly, but the figure on the bridge did not move. He spared a glance at the raging river and rocks below, then looked back to the stoic figure and called out again, but still the figure stood like a statue. It was not until he came to the edge of the bridge did Jonathan push back from the railing and glance over at Stewart, who had stopped at Jonathan's sudden movement.

Approaching warily as he might a wild animal, Stewart walked up the narrow wooden bridge towards Jonathan, who was now once again staring at the churning water below. When he came within a few feet, he heard Jonathan sigh loudly.

"Are you real?"

Stewart paused. "Yes," he said slowly. He down at looked at his arms, then back up to Jonathan. "Do I appear unreal to you?"

Jonathan gave a short laugh that was devoid of humor. "If you are here for retribution, then please push me in now, as I am afraid I am too cowardly to do so myself."

Stewart panted a few times, catching his breath. He wanted to yell at Jonathan, to tell him to stop acting crazily and come back with him. He wanted things back the way they were before Jonathan left, before he had to traipse all over the countryside looking for his friend.

Before that night?

Stewart pushed the thought out of his head. Right now he had to concentrate on getting Jonathan off the bridge and back home. He took another breath before answering in what he considered was an impressive nonchalant voice, given what he was feeling at that moment, "I don't know what you're talking about, ol' chap. I was just looking at the lovely scenery." With that, he turned and rested his elbows on the railing, looking out at the grey and tawny river that cut a wide swath through an equally unattractive brown landscape.

Jonathan scoffed and laughed at the same time, so it came out like a choking sound. He looked up at Stewart, his cheeks wet with tears. Jonathan pinched the bridge of his nose and surreptitiously wiped them away. "Perhaps they'll just write 'coward' as my epitaph and leave it at that."

"Is that what you really think?" Stewart asked, glancing over at Jonathan's tall form. He had lost weight, Stewart could see now; his suit sagged in some places where it had fit snugly before. His face was gaunt, and the usual luster was gone from his hair. But what he could see from his eyes concerned him the most; the fire was gone, the intelligence he had noticed when they were both soldiers was still there, but without the passion.

"Is what what I really think?" Jonathan asked softly.

"Do you really think yourself a coward?"

Jonathan stole a glance at Stewart before looking back at the river. Long moments passed before he spoke. "I cannot do it," he finally said.

"I stood here thinking that all I have to do is step over the edge, but I cannot do it."

"Is that why you had the gun?"

Jonathan put his elbows on the railing and put his head in his hands. "Yes," he muttered. "But then I thought about who would find me, and the mess... someone always has to clean that up, you know. But this way... they may never even find my body. "

"Suicide is a cowardly way out, my friend. It is living that is courageous."

"That is a lie!" Jonathan said, pushing himself upright and putting his hands onto the ledge. "Whoever said that... that... *bull* had no idea-no idea!" He hit the ledge with his hands, accentuating the point. "It is..." he started, then stopped and took a breath. "I can wake up every day and wish to God I were dead," he said in a low, steady voice, "but I cannot take the step to make it happen. So, yes, Stewart, I believe myself to be a coward."

"So the man who saved my life, countless other soldiers' lives, who was awarded not one, but two commendations for bravery, who saved a soldier's home last week, and who provides monetarily for a family who refuses to acknowledge him is a coward?" Stewart paused here, taking a breath before continuing, "Jonathan, the standards you set for yourself make the rest of us look terribly incompetent. Do not go setting your standards even higher- although *you* would most likely qualify for sainthood, I do not believe we would ever be able to catch up."

Jonathan mumbled a few things under his breath about heaven not letting him in that Stewart did not understand, then suddenly gripped the railing and shook his head. "Now you know what I am," he said more clearly.

"What you are? You're my friend."

"You know what. I'm a pansy, a nancy-boy, a batty-boy, a brownie, a-"

"Enough, enough," Stewart said, holding up a hand. "I understand."

Jonathan shook his head. "I cannot be your friend," he muttered.

"Whyever not?

"I cannot... after I did those things to you... how you can stand to look at me..." Jonathan paused for a moment, then continued. "I am dreadfully sorry, you know," he said softly.

"For what now? Did you plot against the crown? Sell out Jesus for 50 pieces of silver? Cause the fall of Rome?"

A reluctant chuckle exploded from Jonathan's lips. "No, none of those. Not that I know of, in any case. Although I may have given a man named Pontius some bad advice."

It was now Stewart's turn to chuckle. "Come, friend, let me take you home," he said.

"No," Jonathan said, grabbing his arm. "I cannot. I am so very sorry. I don't know how you can bear to look at me. I am a monster. Truly, I thought I was dreaming, or I never would have... you have to believe me."

Stewart looked into Jonathan's pleading eyes. "There were two of us in that room, Jonathan," he said very slowly. "What we do with that knowledge will not be determined here, however." He paused for a moment, then continued, "If you wish to grant me a boon, though, I would love to get off of this horrifically rickety bridge which may just collapse at any moment, away from this God-awfully smelling river, and into my very nice carriage."

"It does smell," Jonathan reluctantly agreed, dropping Stewart's arm.

"Come on, Jonathan," Stewart said, pushing back from the railing. "At least let us find an inn that does not smell of cabbage and cheese. There have to be some fine-smelling hotels in Dover."

Jonathan looked down at his boot, rubbing and scuffing off some of the dirt and paint from the bridge. "All right," he sighed. "As it does not appear I'm able to do what I came here for."

Stewart held out an arm, and when Jonathan turned, Stewart grabbed a hold of his hand, squeezing it gently before releasing it and falling in stride with him. "I left my things at the inn," Jonathan murmured, looking at his feet.

"Not an issue. I took your things from your room and put them in the carriage," Stewart told him.

Jonathan looked up. "For what purpose?"

"For very selfish reasons, truly. The inn where you were staying is a rat infested shithole and I do not wish to visit you there."

"Oh. That... is true. I suppose."

"Although, "Stewart said, "I can understand the attraction to the inn."

"You can?" Jonathan asked, surprised.

"Well, I understand Mrs. Beasley makes an excellent tart," he smiled.

Jonathan choked on a laugh as Stewart guided them back to the carriage.

CHAPTER TWENTY-FIVE

Jonathan sighed deeply in the carriage as it came to a stop, contemplating the benefits of an unmarked grave. The trip to Dover had been relatively quiet, with Jonathan spending it staring out the window and Stewart spending it staring at Jonathan. Henry pulled in front of a hotel, and Stewart jumped out almost before the footman had placed the stairs, turning around for Jonathan as he rested on his cane. "Come," he said, motioning to Jonathan, who climbed out reluctantly.

Stewart ordered a bath sent up to the room, telling Jonathan he smelled as quite like the inn, and sent Henry off to fetch Jonathan's trunk. Their room had a large sitting area, with a bedroom off each side.

"Bath first," Stewart ordered, brooking no argument. "You can borrow a shirt and breeches from me, and dress in your own clothing tomorrow."

Jonathan had shrugged, disappearing into the bedroom, and Stewart had listened through the door, making sure Jonathan was not going to bolt. When Jonathan emerged clean and in his borrowed clothing, however, he did not look as if he would go anywhere quickly. Indeed, it appeared that he barely dragged himself into the room.

"It is not too late, but you look tired. Perhaps you should get some sleep, my friend," Stewart said encouragingly.

"I have slept for the past five days," Jonathan sighed. "Truly, I am not sleepy."

"Then eat," Stewart said. "There are no tarts, but I had them bring up several different selections," he said with a smile.

Jonathan was going to tell him he was not hungry, either, but the look on Stewart's face made him close his mouth and head to the sideboard where the dishes were laid out. He knew he was being manipulated, but the guilt over what he had done overrode any arguments he might have made. He filled his plate with one selection of each, and moved to the small table to sit.

Stewart watched him with exacting patience, mentally comparing Jonathan to an abused dog with a bone- afraid to eat, afraid not to eat. Remembering Susanna's words about Jonathan refusing to confront anything head-on, he filled his own plate and sat down across from Jonathan.

"So, I was thinking," Stewart said, "that we should discuss what happened that night."

Jonathan choked on his food- something with egg in it, he believed, and gasped for breath. "What?" he croaked loudly.

"Well," Stewart said calmly- more calmly than he felt, but he hadn't ordered around hundreds of soldiers by sounding fearful, after all, "I do believe that we have two ways of approaching the issue. First, we can pretend it didn't happen, in which case we can return to our previous lives, only every once in a while turning red when someone happens to mention something that reminds us of that evening."

"That one, I choose that one," Jonathan choked out.

"Or," Stewart continued, pretending he didn't hear Jonathan, "we can face it like men, acknowledge what happened, and then make a decision about what to do from there." He speared what he believed to be a potato and popped it into his mouth, waiting.

Jonathan looked down at the food on his plate but did not answer, either in the positive or negative, which Stewart took to be a good sign, as that meant he was at least contemplating the issue. He cleared his plate of food, and pushed up from the table.

"I will leave the time and place of our discussion to you, my friend," he said, made a mock bow to Jonathan, and walked to his bedroom nonchalantly, closing the door behind him. Once inside, however, he sagged into a chair, his heart thundering loudly. He had left word at the front desk that he was to be made aware if Jonathan tried to leave the hotel without him, but still, he was not sure that Jonathan would stay. He closed his eyes and prayed that Jonathan would choose a time to talk sooner rather than later, as he could not keep up his indifferent façade forever.

He knew Jonathan was still berating himself over that kiss. How had he lived for so long near Jonathan, never thinking of him in that way? Well, not really thinking of him like that, anyway. He had always admired Jonathan's wit and intelligence, and certainly he enjoyed looking at him, his fallen angel. Stewart scoffed. Last week was merely the culmination of a thousand different somethings. Until Jonathan had hightailed it out of the room, that was. Stewart closed his eyes, remembering the evening. Life with Jonathan was always complicated.

Jonathan, however, sat dumbfounded in a chair in the next room. Why would Stewart want to talk about what happened? And saying that they could face it like men- wasn't part of being a man ignoring such feelings and pretending they didn't exist? That was what his father had ingrained in him, anyway, and the rest of society was not much better. They would look the other way, of course, as long as he did not flaunt his lifestyle by talking about it, showing any emotion regarding it, or in any other way exposing anyone to any aspect of that part of him. If he failed in that, he faced ridicule, threats to his life, or prison. It was not as if he could really bring such topics up in polite conversation.

Jonathan shook his head, a visible representation of where his thoughts were turning. What was he thinking? Stewart did not really want to be with him- how could he? Jonathan knew Stewart had been with mistresses and other ladies. In truth, however, he had not seen Stewart with a woman since the end of the war, since they had returned to London. But Stewart could not have romantic feelings for him, could he?

Jonathan shook his head to and fro. No, no- Stewart liked women, and he did not. It was quite simple. He should do what Stewart asked, and talk about what happened, apologize again, and let him know that it would never be repeated. That was probably all Stewart needed- a promise that he would never again be subjected to his pawings. And if he *should* happen to come to him in a dream, Jonathan would merely roll over and tell him to go away.

Feeling a bit better, Jonathan stood and walked across the room to Stewart's bedroom and knocked on the door. "Stewart?" he called. "Are you there? Stewart?" He knocked again, but there was no response. He contemplated opening the door, but thought against it. Perhaps Stewart had changed his mind, and no longer wanted to talk? He should just go to his own room and wait until morning, when they could go home. It would be a dashed long carriage ride in any case, and plenty of time for him to apologize then.

CHAPTER TWENTY-SIX

Stewart wondered if he could literally die of frustration when he heard Jonathan's footfalls come closer to his door followed by his hesitant knock. Stewart sighed, pondering what to do, when Jonathan knocked again. He slowly rose and limped to the door.

"Jonathan?" he said, opening the door as Jonathan was turning away.

"Oh, Stewart. Yes, well. I thought it would be best to just say what I need to say and get it out of the way."

"Oh, really?" Stewart raised an eyebrow sardonically. "Is that how a discussion works?"

"No, but- oh, dash it all!" Jonathan said, rubbing his forehead with his hand. "This is too difficult," he muttered.

Stewart frowned. "Close your eyes, Jonathan," he said.

"What? Why?"

"Because I told you to," said Stewart.

Jonathan did not answer, but sighed deeply, and Stewart pulled him into the bedroom. "Now, close your eyes," he repeated.

Jonathan complied, and Stewart placed his hands on either side of Jonathan's face. Jonathan cringed slightly, but did not open his eyes. Stewart took a deep breath, closing his own eyes before leaning forward and gently pressing his lips to Jonathan's.

"Wha?" Jonathan murmured, his eyes flying open. Stewart, however, did not release his face, but deepened the kiss, stepping closer to Jonathan so their bodies were pressed together. Jonathan closed his eyes and kissed Stewart back, gripping Stewart's arms tightly. They stood, kissing, for several moments until Stewart gently eased away.

"Now," he said huskily, "I have kissed you."

Jonathan blinked. "I don't understand," he said. "Does this make us even or something?"

Stewart gave a low chuckle and stepped back. "Come," he said to Jonathan, holding out his hand. Jonathan took it, and Stewart led him towards the bed. "I apologize, but my knee is paining me. I need to put it up."

"Oh, Stewart!" exclaimed Jonathan. "I'll bet you didn't do any of your exercises at all since I left, did you?" He helped Stewart pick his leg up and swung it over, gingerly resting it on the soft bed.

"Come on," said Stewart, patting the area on the bed next to him. "Sit."

"I don't think I should," said Jonathan.

Stewart leveled a look at Jonathan. "Why not? Do you think I'm going to ravish you?"

Jonathan let out a half cry. "Oh, Stewart, I missed you," he wailed.

"And I you, my friend. Come, sit down, and we will talk. Just pretend we are in our chairs in front of the fireplace instead of on a bed."

Jonathan moved to the other side of the bed and slid over. Instead of sitting, however, he lay down next to Stewart, staring up at the white canopy above them. He took a deep breath, not realizing how shallow his breathing had been, and tried to imagine that the past week had not happened; tried to imagine that he was just sitting next to Stewart in the library. The grip on his heart lessened and his breathing became deeper and more even.

"I had quite the adventure this week," Stewart said, breaking the silence. "I thought I was finished with adventure after I retired from the army, but I have met the most interesting people over the past few days."

"Really? Who?" asked Jonathan. "Besides the creepy Mrs. Beadsley, of course."

"She reminded me of that myth," said Stewart.

"Yes, Perseus and the Grey sisters," said Jonathan. "I wonder where the other two are?"

"Perhaps they each run the inn one day a week," said Stewart. "By the way, did you know Mr. Beadsley was dead?"

"Oh, yes," Jonathan said. "But the missus didn't see why she should marry again."

Stewart chuckled. "I also met a fair-haired girl in a quaint little town outside of London."

Jonathan felt his heart clinch. "Really?" he said in the calmest voice he could muster.

"Yes," Stewart said. "That was how I found you, actually."

Jonathan took a shaky breath. "I see," he murmured. "I... I didn't even think how you came to be there, on that bridge. I should have... I should have thought...."

Stewart interrupted him, "Oddly enough, she claimed to be your sister, but I'm fairly certain that she was far too charming to be related to you."

Jonathan chuckled weakly. "I will not argue that point," he said. "What does she look like? Is she pretty?"

"You haven't seen her?" Stewart knitted his eyebrows.

"She was only two when I left," said Jonathan sadly.

Stewart smiled sadly. "Ah, well, yes, she is quite the fetching thing. But what I found interesting was how talkative she was."

Jonathan harrumphed.

"She told me about your father," Stewart said. "And... your lover."

His what? What the hell did Susanna say? "Um..." Jonathan said, thinking frantically for a lie, for some story to tell- any story but the truth.

"She said he betrayed you to your father?"

"The vicar, yes," Jonathan choked.

"What did he say?" Stewart asked softly?

Jonathan drew in a shaky breath. "The vicar or Timothy?"

Stewart felt a stab of jealousy slice through him with the knowledge of the name of Jonathan's mysterious lover. He pushed the feeling down and continued to question Jonathan.

"Either, really. What was the conversation like?"

"Awful, just awful," Jonathan whispered. "Timothy was... an actor. It was all very exciting and fresh and new. I... I believed I loved him, and was planning on leaving with him and the troupe."

"What happened?"

Jonathan shrugged and took a deep breath, trying to keep the tears at bay. "He... had other plans. When the troupe was ready to move on, instead of taking me, he went to the vicar and threatened to expose me for... for what I am." Jonathan's voice caught on the last word and he felt hot tears stream down his face. He covered his face with his hands, hiding his tears from Stewart.

"What's this, now?" said Stewart, "Ah, come now, Jonathan. It's me. You've known me almost half your life. No need to dissemble." He pulled Jonathan close to him, gently stroking his hair.

"I haven't thought about that day in years," Jonathan murmured.

"Good," said Stewart succinctly. "I would hope that thoughts of me have overwhelmed you with such happiness that you no longer find yourself plagued with such horrible memories."

Jonathan gave a tearful laugh. "You sound like me," he said.

"We have rubbed off on one another," Stewart said.

Jonathan did not reply, and several minutes passed, neither breaking the silence. Jonathan did not move his head from Stewart's chest, and soon found himself breathing in rhythm to the steady, easy cadence of Stewart's heart.

"I have thought that you were both my salvation and my penance," Jonathan murmured.

Stewart pursed his lips together. "That sounds quite deep, like something one would say of his mate. We have been carrying on like an old married couple, have we not?" he smiled grimly.

Jonathan chuckled, but a sob caught in his throat. "I just always thought that if I ever... said anything, it would be over. The thought of never seeing you again... truly, I would rather be... dead." Jonathan's voice caught on the last word, and he closed his eyes.

"We can't have that," Stewart said, trying for levity as he squeezed Jonathan around the shoulders gently, "I've put too much time and energy into you. The very thought of training someone new is insufferable."

Jonathan tried to laugh but it came out more like a sob. Stewart sighed and closed his eyes, not knowing what else to say.

"Now what?" Jonathan asked softly, breaking the silence.

Stewart peered down at Jonathan's head with curiosity. "How difficult was that to say?"

"Bloody awful," Jonathan admitted, raising his head and resting on one elbow.

"I imagine," Stewart said, assessing Jonathan's red-rimmed eyes. He pulled Jonathan gently back to his chest.

"Not all of us are able to just... say exactly what's on our minds," Jonathan grumbled.

"That... is true enough, I suppose," said Stewart. "But I want you to work on doing so. It is not healthy to keep so many things bottled up inside of you." Stewart patted Jonathan's arm gently. "Dr. Lambrose was concerned that not expressing yourself is a reason for your weak heart."

Jonathan gave a sarcastic laugh. "Dr. Lambrose and his temperance ways can go to the devil. In any case, what was I supposed to do?"

"You could have told me... well, *something*."

"Oh, yes," Jonathan said, pulling away from Stewart and lying on his back next to him. "I should have expressed myself sooner about my immoral urges. I'm sure you would have still invited me to live with you and work for you," he said sarcastically. He put an arm over his face and sniffed. "I would have been kicked out of the townhouse and jailed."

Stewart frowned. "Do you really think that?"

Jonathan shrugged.

Several minutes passed before Stewart broke the silence, "Have you really been in love with me all this time? For the past 15 years?"

Jonathan gave a short laugh in spite of himself, choking a bit, and sat up. Stewart reached over his head and grabbed a handkerchief from the nightstand, passing it over to Jonathan, who gratefully accepted it, wiping his nose and face before stuffing it into his breeches pocket. Without thinking, he lay back down and put his head back on Stewart's chest.

"Thank you," he said.

"Of course," Stewart answered simply, lightly stroking Jonathan's back through his shirt. "But Jonathan, you knew about my... well, my mistresses, my lovers. Why did you bother to stay?"

"I... well, I love you," Jonathan stammered.

"But, Jonathan, well... 15 years. Are you to tell me you have not been with anyone else in 15 years?"

Jonathan looked up and shook his head slightly. "No," he whispered.

Stewart's eyebrows raised. "Really? Not once?"

Jonathan frowned. "It's not as if it is something one can advertise, you know," he scoffed. "In the army it could have gotten me killed. In London I'd just get beaten up or thrown into jail."

Stewart sighed deeply but did not answer.

"Besides," Jonathan continued after a few moments. "I said you were my penance."

"Penance?" Stewart asked. "I don't understand."

"For, well, for being born... *that way.*"

Stewart scooted back on the bed cushions to get a better view of Jonathan. "Wait- let me get this straight. You thought that falling in love with me was... what... *punishment?*"

"I didn't mean it like that," Jonathan grumbled.

"Bloody well better not have," Stewart said. "Punishment indeed." They sat there in silence until Stewart added, "Besides, you have done nothing whatsoever to deserve punishment. Well, besides being a bore when I try to teach you whist."

Jonathan smiled wanly and rubbed his eyes. "I never knew it meant that much to you."

"Well, I find out you've been in love with me for 15 years, and I could have used that as incentive all this time. Bloody waste of information I could have used to my advantage. But never fear- now that I know, I will act accordingly," Stewart gave Jonathan a little shake to let him know he was joking.

"I'm going to kill Susanna," Jonathan frowned.

Stewart chuckled. "She's a very lively young lass. She loves you, you know."

"I suppose," Jonathan admitted, "Although she doesn't really know me. It's not as if I could ever go back."

"No, no I suppose not," Stewart said. "Did you know that my sister is sponsoring her next Season?" he added.

Jonathan could not stop the small laugh that came out of his mouth. "Susanna told you?"

"Oh, yes," Stewart smiled. "I want to be there, you know."

"Be there when?"

"When you convince my sister that it was her idea to sponsor Miss Redding."

"Yes, well... she probably needs a project, you know."

"Otherwise what else would she spend her time doing?"

"Exactly," Jonathan smiled, closing his eyes. He could hear the steady beat of Stewart's heart through his linen shirt. Bum-bump, bum-bump, a constant beacon that steadied him. He felt himself getting drowsy.

"You know, we will eventually have to discuss this... thing," Stewart said, gently shaking Jonathan from slumber.

Jonathan blinked his eyes open. No, that was the last thing in the world he wished to do. He wanted to stay like this, forever, holding Stewart close, breathing in his strong sandalwood cologne, listening to his strong heart beat a steady tattoo that had was imprinted upon his soul. No, talking was the last thing he wanted to do.

"Tell me what you think," Jonathan hedged, and felt his breath catch.

"Honestly?" Stewart replied, "I don't know. This..." he waved his free arm, "is all quite new to me. The idea... of this... is not something I ever truly considered."

"So what, then?" Jonathan said, confused.

"I guess... I think we will have to take it day by day. I am not sure what conclusion I'll come to... that *we'll* come to. But we *will* have to talk about it."

"I don't feel comfortable talking about it," Jonathan said. "I've spent my entire life *not* talking about it."

"Well I know it," Stewart chuckled. "But in this I must insist."

Jonathan sighed and slightly burrowed his cheek deeper into Stewart's chest. Stewart looked down and gave a small smile, gently hugging Jonathan closer.

"Maybe we can talk about something else first and work up to it?" Jonathan suggested. Like his love of trees. They should plant more trees at the country house. Like apple trees. Yes, trees were safe to discuss.

"Very well," Stewart said slowly. "How is it that you suffer from melancholia, and you never bothered to tell me?"

For God's sake, Susanna! "It's not something one brings up in polite conversation, you know," Jonathan said testily.

"Polite-? Jonathan, we have known each other for 15 years. We've fought together, we live together. We have gone far beyond polite conversation," Stewart replied in equally clipped tones.

Jonathan did not respond, and Stewart sighed deeply. "I have a feeling that this is going to be a process, my friend. But there is one thing you must promise me."

"What?" Jonathan said, pushing himself up and leveling his eyes at Stewart, who gave him a sad smile.

"You cannot rush off again. If not for your health, then for mine."

Jonathan frowned and put his head back down onto Stewart's chest. "I suppose," he muttered.

"Jonathan?" Stewart shook him gently. "Jonathan?"

"What?" Jonathan said, pushing himself up again, looking directly at Jonathan. "I said yes."

"No, you said that you supposed. That is not a yes. But that is not what I wanted to clarify."

"What?" Jonathan snapped, his eyes angry.

"When I say you cannot rush off, I mean that you are not to leave me again. Ever." Stewart stared straight into Jonathan's deep blue eyes, searching for something he knew not what.

Jonathan's eyes softened and a hint of a smile touched his face. "All right then," he said softly, putting his head back down onto Stewart's chest and holding him close. "I suppose."

Stewart chuckled and they once again were bathed in silence. "You know, in all of the excitement I never did tell you what I had decided to call the school," he said.

"Stewart's School?"

"Please tell me you will never start a business without running the name by me first."

"All right," Jonathan yawned. "Pray tell, what is the illustrious name you're giving to your legacy?"

"I've decided to call it Redding's School for Boys."

Jonathan went very still before swallowing hard. "That's... I..." he said.

"I believe one of the requirements of the school is that everyone must read the dictionary."

Jonathan did not say anything, merely sniffed.

"You'll have to use the handkerchief I just gave you," Stewart smiled. "I don't have another one handy."

"That's... that's the nicest thing I can think anyone has ever done for me," Jonathan finally said.

"You mean, besides travel back and forth across the countryside looking for you?"

"Well, yes," Jonathan said. "Besides that."

"And don't make me do it again," Stewart warned.

"I said I wouldn't," Jonathan muttered against his shirt. "But would you? Not that I would. But let's just say I did."

Stewart smiled, and patted Jonathan's head reassuringly. "In a heartbeat, my friend," he said. "I would follow you to the ends of the earth, as you well know."

"Good," mumbled Jonathan. "A chap has to hear that sometimes, you know."

Many hours later, Stewart woke to find himself on his side, Jonathan holding him from behind. The light of predawn was starting to peek through the shutters. "Mmm," he muttered. "I should probably go to the other bedroom and let you sleep."

"No. Stay," Jonathan murmured against his neck, pressing a gentle kiss to his skin.

Stewart took in a deep breath. For as long as he had known Jonathan, fought alongside Jonathan, worked with Jonathan, Jonathan had never directly demanded anything. Until now.

"I will," Stewart whispered, and Jonathan sighed contently, pulling him closer before settling back into sleep.

EPILOGUE

It had been a grey, dismal day when Stewart had watched his friend's coffin lowered into the ground. Although the sun had not come out, it was not raining. Jonathan would have liked that.

There were few mourners; Jonathan had never been one to make many friends, but besides the servants, Susanna, her husband and children were there to watch the funeral, even though women were usually not present during the burial. Jonathan would have appreciated the flaunting of society's expectations, thought Stewart with some amusement.

Now, a week after he had put his friend to rest, Stewart was there to supervise the tombstone as it was raised over Jonathan's grave. Stewart lightly fingered the carved marble before his nephew came around to the back of his chair. "Ready, Uncle?" he asked.

"Just a moment," Stewart said. "He was obsessed with this, you know. Agonized for years about what it would say."

His nephew offered him a sad smile. "He was a good man," he said.

"Yes, he was," Stewart sighed. "And he is probably at heaven's gate right now, his toe tapping, saying, 'Where the devil are you? You're late!'" Stewart coughed and began to wheeze heavily, sitting back into the chair with a soft thud.

"Uncle?"

"I'm... I'm alright," Stewart finally caught his breath and gave a low chuckle. "I don't think he'll have to wait for much longer. But I had to last for this day, to make sure that they did it right, you know. Because it was important to him."

"Of course, Uncle," his nephew said to placate him. "You did your duty by him, however. I know he served with you in the war, and he worked as your secretary- but really... you took care of him for over 40 years. The man was- what? I think 75 years old? I think a tombstone is a bit superfluous."

"You think he would like it?" Stewart blurted out.

"I do not believe he could have come up with anything more appropriate," his nephew answered honestly.

"Truly, I think not," Stewart sighed contentedly. "Very well then, we can go back to the house, I suppose."

Stewart fingered the tombstone again before motioning to his nephew to take him away, but looked back on it one last time:

Jonathan Wilson Redding
1780-1855
"Beloved Brother and Cherished Friend"

NOW AVAILABLE
BY ELIZABETH MAY

MUCH ADO ABOUT THE SHREW

A dying promise to protect her...
Benedick Barrett's only real problem growing up was that he was named after a character in a Shakespeare play. After his best friend is shot in a senseless duel, Benedick Barrett makes his dying friend a promise to watch over his sister, who just happens to also be named after the heroine in the same play, and whom he has always hated. When Benedick returns to London after the Napoleonic Wars, however, he finds himself having to escort his nemesis Beatrice from ballroom to ballroom. Benedick finds himself attracted to the very woman he has despised for years, and if that weren't enough, the very man who killed Beatrice's brother returns to London to claim Beatrice for his own! Benedick must struggle through his own feelings before Beatrice, and his very happiness, is lost to him forever.

****

THE DEVOTED VAMPIRE

He was dangerous to everyone but her...
Lisa is a mild-mannered researcher with severe asthma and a lack of potential love interests. When her date abandons her on the side of the road in the rain, she is hopeful that someone will come to her aid, but she gets more than she bargained for when a vampire stops and rescues her. The question is, does he see her as a potential mate... or a potential meal?

NOW AVAILABLE FOR SALE AND DOWNLOAD!

Printed in Great Britain
by Amazon